Words Don't Come Forth

J.M. McKenzie

Michael Andrews

S.J. Gibbs

JAMS Publishing

Copyright © 2021 JAMS Publishing

The authors of this anthology retain all copyrights to their pieces of work, characters and places.

All Rights Reserved. No part of this publication may be reproduced, stored in a retrieval system, or transmitted, in any form or by any means, electronic, mechanical, photocopying, recording or otherwise without the prior consent of the author.

This anthology is a work of fiction. The names, characters and incidents portrayed in it are the work of the authors' imaginations. Any resemblance to actual persons, living or dead, or events that have occurred are entirely coincidental.

ISBN: 9798785773257

CONTENTS

	Introduction	Pg 1
48	Herman Sligo	Pg 11
49	We went as far as the car could take us	Pg 33
50	Darryl and the vending machine	Pg 61
51	Carlos and the closet	Pg 77
52	Lena	Pg 107
53	So it was all just a lie	Pg 131
54	Who was Paul Fischer	Pg 153
55	Johnnie's Murder	Pg 177
56	Once upon a time	Pg 193
57	Jannette or Jeannette	Pg 209
58	A cuddle from Libbie	Pg 233
59	Alone	Pg 247
	A Message from the Authors and Bibliographies	Pg 263

ACKNOWLEDGMENTS

To Mike and Stephen. Thanks for putting up with the after effects of the writers group meetings.

.

Introduction.

Our group was formed in the spring of 2015, when we existed as DH Writers Group with the sole aim of supporting each other to develop our writing careers. In 2019, we made the decision to extend that support to other aspiring writers, and we developed our hobby into a small business, changing our name to JAMS Publishing as part of the process. We now offer proof-reading and editing, critiquing and self-publishing support. We also run writing competitions.

Please visit our website at
https://www.jamspublishing.com to find out more.

In terms of our own development as writers, for each meeting we write a short piece of fiction utilising a randomly selected brief/writing prompt. In 2018, we published three years' worth of the outputs of this exercise in our first anthology, "Words Don't Come Easy". Our second book, "Words Don't Come *Two* Easy" picked up from where the previous book left off and contains our work from mid-2018 until mid-2019. Our third anthology, "Words Don't Come Threely" brings together our collective work from mid-2019 until the end of 2020. This fourth anthology works through our assignments written during a challenging 2021. All four books are available on Amazon, in both Kindle and paperback formats.

In the first anthology, the majority of our prompts were taken from a book which Michael had found on Amazon, "1000 Awesome Writing Prompts" by Ryan Andrew Kinder. We would urge other aspiring writers (or groups) to purchase and try out this book to challenge and inspire themselves. (It's available on Amazon). In 2019, after pretty much exhausting Ryan's ideas and feeling that we needed a change, we started using prompts from "The First Line" (https://www.thefirstline.com/), who publish collections of stories that all begin with the same first line. Halfway through this year, as part of expanding our JAMS Publishing business, we took the decision to start making our own prompts. Each month, we would make five prompts each and into a hat they went! The aim for next year is to produce our own writing prompt book to help other aspiring writers take that first step.

We read our work aloud at our meetings, offering constructive criticism in a safe environment. In 2019, we also started undertaking written critiques for each other, using the detailed framework that AJ developed to judge our competition entries. These critiques are not shared with the group and we have given each other permission to be completely honest without concerns about causing hurt or offence. This has worked well so far, and enables us to give much more considered, and sometimes more challenging, feedback than was possible in the open group setting.

As with the previous three publications, this book presents our stories in date order accompanied by some of our thoughts and observations. The pieces are published as they were on the day they were read at the meeting and have not been edited or corrected. In this way, the book should reflect our individual journeys as writers over the past few years.

The group currently has three core members, and this book contains their work only. Other members have come and gone but their work is not included in this compilation. The three core members are J.M. McKenzie, Michael Andrews and S.J. Gibbs. What follows is a short biography written by each writer.

At the end of the book is a bibliography of the writers' works, and in the kindle version, hyperlinks will take you to the respective product pages.

J.M. McKenzie

J.M. had a long career in healthcare but, like many people, always had a personal ambition to write a book. As a child she aspired to be a writer but was never encouraged or supported to follow this career path. She always wrote in the context of her work, but this was largely on commercial and scientific subjects. It was only after she took early retirement in 2018 that she started writing in earnest.

Her first ever full-length publication was in 2020 and was a non-fiction biography, *My Rachel,* that she was proud to co-author with S.J. Gibbs. This is a personal memoir of the lives of S.J. and her daughter, Rachel, who was born with severe cerebral palsy. Rachel is now in her thirties, and the book recounts the relationship between mother and daughter and their fight for life, truth and justice.

In January 2021 she published her first fictional novel, *Wait for Me*, the extraordinary story of one ordinary woman's journey to get home to her husband at the start of the zombie apocalypse in the UK. *Trident Edge*, the sequel to *Wait for Me*, was published in October 2021.

J.M. has also published two short stories. *Puschkinia*, published in 2019, is a gentle tale about a lost wedding ring and the role of an innocent child in breaking down prejudice and misunderstanding.

The Each Uisage, published in 2021, is a spooky Scottish

folklore tale, inspired by a trip to the Outer Hebrides.

In 2020, she got through to Round 2 of the NYC Midnight Short Story Challenge with her entry in the spy genre called, *Option 3*.

In 2021 she got through to Round 2 of the NYC Flash Fiction Challenge with her stories, *The Buttonologist* and *From Venice with Love*.

She is currently debating with herself on whether to develop an idea for a completely new dystopian, post-apocalyptic novel, or whether to tell another story from the UK zombie apocalypse.

Website:https://jswritingservices.com/blog/

Facebook:JSWS

Instagram:jswritingservices

Twitter:@JMMcKenzie1

Michael Andrews

Michael Andrews had always dreamed about writing a novel, ever since a school assignment at the age of 14 was writing the start to a book. An avid reader of fantasy and science fiction, Michael's imagination was stretched by the likes of David Eddings, Raymond E Feist and Orson Scott Card.

However, it was only after a thirty year career in logistics and planning that Michael finally sat himself down and started his first novel in earnest. With the advent of the Kindle, Amazon opened up the doorway to independent authors and nine months later, Michael's first child, "For The Lost Soul" was published. A poetry collection inspired by the bullying theme within For The Lost Soul soon followed, receiving recognition with publishing within The Canon's Mouth, The Bully Book by Alisha Paige, reaching the final of the Mary Charman-Smith Poetry competition and finally, "The Empty Chair" was published.

Wishing to write a shorter read, but still keeping a long term plot in process, Michael started work on a series of novels, "The Alex Hayden Chronicles" with titular character Alex, a thousand year old vampire trapped forever in the body of a fourteen year old boy. Set in modern day Blackpool, he teams up with Detective Harry Shepherd to stop a serial killer in the first volume, "Under A Blood Moon". The series is now complete with "The Howling Wind", "The Cauldron of Fire", "Dragonfire" and "Children of the Sun".

Michael also has written a behind the scenes book about his journey during the series called "Being Alex Hayden".

As well as his own publications, Michael has been featured in "Cathartic Screams" by Severance Publishing, "The Bully Book" by Alisha Paige and "The Canons Mouth"

S.J. Gibbs

S.J.'s love of reading and writing started at a very young age and as a teenager would often be found with her nose in a book and used to read under the bedclothes with a torch after her father used to turn out her bedroom light. After leaving school, in her spare time, she wrote short stories for her own pleasure. Reading was still her passion.

In 1987, her first daughter was born and diagnosed with profound cerebral palsy. This prompted her to start writing a novel about the struggles of bringing up a daughter with a severe disability. However, she was forced to stop work on this when the emotions involved in the project became too much for her.

At the beginning of 2015, S.J.'s writing began in earnest, after she joined Michael, Jackie and Anita in the writer's group. Here she found a new love of writing fiction. Encouraged by J.M., she undertook The Writers Bureau Creative Writing Course, which she has since completed and thoroughly enjoyed.

She contributed to a collaborative novel and a series of anthologies started by the group. While the group were compiling an anthology, Michael encouraged S.J. to write a short story so that she could experience the joy of publishing her own work. *Fighting A Battle With Himself* was published on Amazon in 2018.

in 2020, she had another attempt at telling her daughter's story, this time with Jackie's help and support. *My Rachel* was published in December 2020

In 2021, she published her first fictional novel, *The Cutting Edge*, the story of one girl's struggle to overcome many hurdles to reach her goal of becoming an Olympic ice skater.

Later in 2021 she published *A Parallel Persona*, an thoughtful and sometimes disturbing examination of one woman's complex emotional reaction to a tragic event.

JAMS Publishing

Assignment Forty Eight - Herman Sligo was a bit actor who played Uncle Emil in three episodes of the popular television series The Five Sisters

30th October 2020

J.M. showed her skill at introducing humour into a serious story, charting a chain of events and how something simple can have spiralling consequences.

Michael enjoyed adding an unexpected twist into his story, something which he is eager to do more of.

S.J. turned her hand to romance, in an effort to expand her repertoire and shows in her story that honesty can pay dividends.

Herman

by

J. M. McKenzie

Herman wants to leave his mark on the world. With each passing day this seems less and like likely. But maybe the mark he leaves won't be the one he is expecting.

Herman Sligo was a bit actor who played Uncle Emil in three episodes of the popular television series, The Five Sisters. Herman had always wanted to leave his mark on the world but unfortunately, he was coming to terms with the fact that this wasn't going to happen. At least not in the way he'd hoped. Uncle Emil, far from being the role that kickstarted his big TV career, appeared to have signalled its decline. The character had been written out of the show and, despite numerous auditions, he'd not had a sniff of a part for approaching 18 months now.

In fact, it was when he was heading home one dreary and dismal Thursday afternoon in early October, after yet another humiliating, and frankly depressing, audition, that he had his encounter with Elizabeth Lawrence. He wasn't looking where he was going. His head was down, partly to shield his face from the lashing rain, but mostly because he was pondering his increasingly tenuous financial situation. His savings had long-since run out, he was behind on his rent and had received letters from all his utility providers, threatening to cut him off if he ignored their most recent payment demands. The whole world seemed grey to Herman. The wet pavement beneath his feet, the towering office blocks on either side of the street, and the gloomy sky above him. All grey. Like his mood. Dark grey edging towards black.

***

Elizabeth Lawrence was buoyant. She had just sealed the deal of her life. She felt as though she was walking on air as she made her way down Headington Avenue, coffee in one hand, phone in the other, to meet Ray for a celebratory lunch-time drink. She didn't see the middle-aged man step out from the side street until it was too late. He stepped out in right front of her and they collided with a crash.

"Hey!" Elizabeth looked down at her blouse which was now stained with decaf, skinny, soya latte. "Watch where you're going buddy!"

The man looked at her in total confusion. His once handsome, jowly face was creased with worry lines. His greying hair was thin and swept across his head in a ridiculous comb-over. He took a moment to orientate himself then he looked at her blouse.

"Jeez! I'm sorry! My fault. Wasn't looking. Things on my mind you know."

Elizabeth felt a pang of remorse for the way she had yelled at him. He looked broken. Worn out.

"it's ok buddy. No real harm done. Just a spot of coffee. I can sponge it out."

She darted into the nearby department store. Through

the window Herman saw her talk to an assistant, who ducked beneath the counter and came back up with a plastic bottle and a wad of tissue. *No harm done. Just a spot of coffee.*

He's been so deep in thought he'd lost track of where he was. He looked up at the street sign. Headington and 8th. Two more blocks and he'd be home. With one last look at Elizabeth, who was now dabbing at her blouse with the tissues, he carried on his way.

Neither of them saw Elizabeth's cell phone, with its glittery case and shattered screen, lying in the gutter.

***

Ray waited at McGinty's as long as he could. 12.30 she'd said. A quick drink she'd said. Something important to tell him. Damn her. It was now 1.15 and she wasn't even answering her cell. He had been due back at the office for 1. Now he was going to have to work over. Anne was going to be pissed! It was his turn to take Junior to football practice. Damn her. Damn them both. Why was his life so complicated?

***

Anne was livid. It was Ray's turn to take Junior to football practice and he was late. Again! Now she was going to miss book club. Again! He was "working late" a lot lately. She was sure he was up to his old tricks. Well, this was the last time. No more second chances. This time she was going to end it for good. She would have to call Julie to tell her she wasn't going to make book club coz it was supposed to be her turn to drive. Julie wouldn't mind. She was a sweetheart.

***

"I don't have to go bowling, Jules. You have the car. I know how much you love your book club."

"Oh Bob, but you hardly *ever* go out. I *want* you to go. To have a good time. You deserve it. I'll be ok. If you could drop me there on your way, I'll get one of the other girls to give me a ride home."

"If you're sure, Hun? I'm not gonna lie. I've been looking forward to seeing the guys."

"I'm sure. Honestly! It'll be fine. I sure hope Anne's ok. She sounded really stressed on the phone."

"That Ray of hers is a bit of a douche. I've heard talk about him and none of its good. Believe me! No wonder she's stressed.

"Oh, poor Anne. It must be so tough. Come on, darling. We're gonna have to leave early if you're gonna get there in time."

***

Sue had just pulled out of the parking lot after book club when her car headlights picked out a woman walking down the sidewalk. It had been raining all day and now it was blowing a gale, *and* it was pitch black and freezing. The woman had her collar up and her coat pulled tightly around her. What in God's name was she doing out there?

She slowed down as she passed and wound down the passenger window.

"Are you ok ... Julie! What are you doing? Where's your ride?"

"Oh, Sue. Anne was due to drive tonight and she couldn't come and Bob's gone bowling."

"Why didn't you say? Get in! You can't walk home in this weather!"

She leaned over and opened the door. Julie climbed in rubbing her arms against the cold.

"It's colder than I thought! Thanks Sue. I really don't want to be a trouble."

"It's no trouble. But why didn't you say?"

"I didn't like to ask. I know everyone's so busy. Rushing home to their families an' all."

"Not too busy to give you ride on a wicked night, Julie. Come on. Where do you live?"

"Blake Street, 712."

"Jeez that's miles away!"

"I know. I'm sorry!"

"No, no! I didn't mean it like that! I meant miles for

you! I can't believe you were going to walk all that way!"

"Oh, I'm used to walking, Sue it ... "

"Nonsense! It's way too far. I'll have you home in 10 minutes."

"Thanks, Sue. It's so kind of you."

***

Leo was on the late shift at the Seven Eleven. He hated working the late shift. In his eyes, anyone who came out shopping after midnight had to be up to no good. Who in their right mind would be picking up groceries in an area like this after dark? And the weather tonight was shit. Pouring rain and a howling gale. Yeah, you'd have to be either mad or bad to come out on a night like this. Ok, so he had security cameras and a button to push under the counter that linked directly to the cop station a couple of blocks away. And yeah, he had a Colt 1911 tucked in a drawer next to the till, just in case. But still, it was gonna be long night.

Some car headlights pulled into the lot out front. *Here we go. Mad or bad?* Leo thought.

The bell above the door jangled as a well-dressed, middle aged woman bustled into the shop. *Mad for sure.*

She headed straight for the cooler, grabbed a carton of milk, and brought it over to the counter.

"Is that all?" Leo asked.

"Yeah. Thanks."

"Two dollars ninety please?"

The woman rifled in her purse.

"Haven't see you in here before." Leo said, trying to sound friendly. This might be the only decent conversation he'd have in the next nine hours.

She looked up and smiled, as if seeing him for the first time. "No. I'm out of my way. Gave a friend a ride home. Needed some milk." She waved the carton at him.

"Ah. Thought I didn't recognise you."

The door jangled again.

***

Jake wasn't sure where he was. Both literally and figuratively. He'd been off his meds for weeks now and he was drifting in and out of lucidity. Sometimes the voices were quiet and he'd be able to think clearly for long enough to decide to go home and sort himself out, then they'd all start talking again telling him not go home, not to take is meds, not to trust his Mom, his doctor, or anyone for that matter. There were so many of them, all talking at once, and they were so loud and all telling him to do different things, to go there, to come here, to look out for this person or that person. Eventually, he'd blank out for a while and come to somewhere with no idea how he got there.

That was how he found himself outside the Seven Eleven. It was the only building around with any lights on. He was tired and thirsty, but he had no money. He stood and watched it for a while from across the street. A car pulled up and a woman got out and hurried inside. He saw her pick something up and take it to the counter. It looked like milk. Ice-cold, creamy white milk. He saw himself opening the carton and pouring its soothing contents down his parched throat. He walked purposely over to the store.

***

Leo stopped talking and stared at the guy that had just walked in. Sue saw the look of concern that swept over his features and turned around. She gasped. A man, or boy (it was impossible to tell), stood in the doorway. Wild eyes stared out from a face that was streaked with filth. His long hair and beard were unwashed and matted. She could smell him from where she stood. His ragged clothes were several sizes too big for him and held together with lengths of cord.

He stepped towards her and reached for her purse. Instinctively, she looked around for a weapon. Her eyes rested on a large glass bottle of cordial. She snatched at it and swung it at the man's head in one movement. He dropped like stone. As he fell, she thought she heard him say something. Just one word. It sounded like *milk*.

***

Jake woke up in the ER an hour later. He was on a gurney with green paper curtains pulled around him. He was wearing a hospital gown and was naked underneath.

His head hurt. The voices were louder than ever. *Get out! Get out! Run! Hide! They're going to kill you.*

Jake got out. He leapt off the trolley and ran. He ran straight out of the double doors ahead into a corridor beyond. Someone shouted after him.

"Hey! Where you going? Wait!"

He didn't wait. Ahead of him, a set of elevator door opened, and a nurse got out. She looked at him briefly but walked briskly away. He got in. The doors closed. *Go up! Go high! Get to the top.* He pushed the button for the 6th floor.

***

Alice Mayer was working in the VIP suite at the Walter Reed Medical Centre. She loved working up there on the 6th floor away from the hustle and bustle of the rest of the hospital. Only one patient to look after. Lots of hot security guys to feast her eyes on and even try to flirt with a little. She was spectacularly unsuccessful in the flirting department though. She suspected this had as much to with the cold professionalism of her targets, as it had the biohazard suit that concealed her ample curves and tiny waste, and the PPI equipment that covered her entire face except for her soft brown eyes.

She was in the treatment room, drawing up some medications, 10ml of potassium chloride to insert into his IV to correct his hypokalaemia, and 10mls of remdesvir to deliver as an IV bolus. She was just about to stick the red warning sticker on the potassium syringe, when she heard a commotion outside. She went to the door just in time to see the security men wrestling, what looked like a homeless guy back into the elevator. She tutted and went back into the room.

Darn it! Which one was the potassium? She looked at the two identical syringes of clear liquid. She was pretty sure the one on the left was the potassium. She had drawn up the remdesvir first and put it down on her right. Yes! She was sure. The one on the left was the potassium. She stuck the sticker on the syringe and put them both on the tray. She left the treatment room and walked down the corridor to her patient.

Donald John Trump died at 11pm on Thursday the 3rd of October 2020, after being accidentally administered a lethal dose of IV potassium chloride by bolus injection, while in hospital being treated for Covid-19.

Herman Sligo climbed into bed after another miserable day in what was proving to be the longest run of miserable days in his entire life. He'd always wanted to leave his mark on the world, but he was beginning to feel as through that was never going to happen. But he wasn't giving up just yet. In the words of Scarlett O'Hara, "After all, tomorrow is another day."

Herman and Jessica

By

Michael Andrews

Having lost his dream role, actor Herman Sligo spirals out of control. His love has turned to hatred and he is presented with a chance to confront the superstar who was responsible for ruining his life.

Herman Sligo was a bit actor who played Uncle Emil in three episodes of the popular television series The Five Sisters. He had been so excited to get the role as it would mean that he got to meet his idol, Jessica Holliday. The sixteen-year-old global icon was a beautiful, slim actress and a great singer to boot and Herman had a secret crush on her, despite her age.

The first day on set, forty-five-year-old Herman had nervously approached her, offered a shaky hand and stammered a greeting. He had dreamed of the meeting for the six weeks after landing the ongoing role of Uncle Emil and he knew that they would bond instantly.

However, to prove the old adage that you should never meet your heroes, Jessica disdainfully looked down her nose at the oily haired actor, sniffed at his greeting and turned away, calling over her make-up artist to provide an escape route.

Herman was crushed but for three weeks, he tried to win her over, showering her with flowers and small gifts that he left in her dressing room. Unfortunately, when he crept into leave his latest gift, she was in the process of getting undressed and he came face to face with a very upset naked teenager. With her shrill complaints ringing in everyone's ears, the producers quickly wrote Herman out of the show and his name was blacklisted amongst the acting community.

His life spiralled into an alcoholic and drug fuelled depression and he spent his days staring up at the posters on the walls of his studio apartment, or watching concerts or films of Jessica, his secret longing for her, and her rejection of him festering away in his mind. Every day, he re-watched those three episodes where he was with her, how she had kissed his cheek, how he had touched her arm or put his arm around her slim waist.

"If only she had seen how much I love her, it would all have been different," Herman muttered to himself as he started his fourth large tumbler of whisky. He heard the steady tick tick of the large white wall clock; its' comforting beat was a steady reminder that he was still alive, and he glanced over to see what the time was.

"Ten thirty," he mumbled. "I guess I ought to get dressed."

Scratching himself through his crumpled, stained boxer shorts, he lurched to his feet, slipping once, before steadying himself on the tatty brown sofa. Rubbing his now bruised hip, he screwed up his nose.

"What the fuck is that smell?" Having a look around his small lounge cum kitchenette for a dead animal, he soon realised that it was the stench of his own body. Picking up a dingy looking dishcloth, Herman wiped his armpits in a futile attempt to mask the smell. Giving up, he opened the fridge. Mouldy bacon stared back at him and upon lifting the lid of the bread bin, he gagged as the smell of a very green loaf hit his nostrils.

'In other news, Jessica Holliday will be appearing at Great Western Mall later this afternoon to perform her latest single, and to meet her fans.'

"What?" Herman's face lit up and he scrambled over to the chair. Gazing lovingly at the images on screen, he made his mind up that he had to see her. "This is it. This is my chance to tell her what I think of her, to show her what she did to me."

With new purpose, Herman showered, picking himself up from the slippery tiles five times. He washed himself with coarse soap until his skin burned with the rawness that he had scrubbed into his body. Wiping the condensation from the mirror, he stared at his unshaven face as his shaking hand picked up the razor. Ten minutes and a few curse words later, he had stopped most of the bleeding and he winced as he splashed copious amounts of aftershave on his freshly peeled face.

"I need to find the perfect clothes," Herman laughed manically to himself, feeling brighter than he had in months. He opened his wardrobe and swooshed his hanging clothes back and forth. Dressed in a pale blue shirt and dark blue denim jeans, he picked up his keys and jacket before noticing his Colt 45 pistol on the sideboard. Slipping on the holster, he secured the handgun, put his jacket on and zipped it up and left his apartment to meet his destiny.

Jessica waved at her beloved and adoring fans as she finished her brand new song. They had loved it, and she revelled in the love that they showed her. Stepping down from the temporary stage, the throng of people, both young and old, pressed forwards, trying to touch her, to reach her, to feel like they were part of her world. She knew that it was part of the job and she had her image to uphold, that of the girl next door, America's favourite daughter. She had played the role perfectly since she had burst onto the scene aged just eleven, when she landed the role of Amelie, in the Five Sisters.

Now, having just turned seventeen, she had moved from the girl next door image into one of blossoming sexuality, and she played on it perfectly. In public at least. Privately she hated the creepy letters and pictures that fans sent, especially older men. She made it past the crowd and headed back to a staff room which was being used for her changing room.

She shuddered for a moment as she recalled being caught naked in her dressing room by that pervert who had played her "Uncle Emil". While she was lost in her memories, she felt herself bumped and looked up. A man in a pale shirt was standing in front of her, a red baseball cap pulled down, covering his face from any security camera.

"You fucking bitch!" the man snarled at her and time slowed down as he reached inside a black leather jacket. Her eyes flicked up and met his. Recognition ran through her brain as she saw a man that she had been so afraid of for a number of months.

"How did you get past security?" she whimpered as her legs started to shake. "What do you want?"

"You ruined my life, you little cock tease!" the man hissed. "You said that you loved me."

"That was on the show," she cried. "It was Amelie."

"You are Amelie, you stupid bitch!" The man's hand shook as he raised the gun. "But no longer!"

Jessica waited for the shot and heard a man's voice shout "NOOOO!"

The crack of the gun sounded like a firecracker and she felt as though her body had suddenly been hit by a car and she fell to the ground. She waited for the pain of the bullet wound to register but she felt nothing.

Voices of her security team filled the dim corridor and there was the sound of bodies hitting the ground. She opened her eyes to see the leather jacket man face down, his arms twisted behind his back.

"Jessica; are you okay?" a weak voice said.

She looked to her left and her eyes widened. "Herman?" There was an expanding patch of red on his pale blue shirt. "Oh my God! Herman! Are you okay?"

She crawled over to him and looked into his eyes. His dark brown eyes stared back, tears leaking down his cheeks.

"I'm so sorry about what happened," Herman croaked out. "I just wanted to tell you that I..."

"Shush," Jessica said, stroking his cheek as she watched the light from his eyes fade. She leaned down and kissed the cheek of the man who had just saved her life.

The chapel was full. Father Keith stood to one side as he gave way to the beautiful young actress whose face was etched in sorrow. Jessica looked up at the waiting mass, and the cameras of the world's media.

Taking a deep breath, she began her eulogy.

"Herman Sligo played my Uncle Emil for just three episodes in The Five Sisters…"

False Impressions

By

S.J. Gibbs

Herman Sligo was a bragger, he couldn't help himself. He'd built a life, he couldn't afford after experiencing a little bit of celebrity status. Love and affection had never entered his life until now, or had it?

Herman Sligo was a bit actor who played Uncle Emil in three episodes of the popular television series The Five Sisters.

He wished he hadn't bragged about being a famous actor, as he now had to make up lies to cover what his big mouth had spurted out. He'd made himself sound like an 'A' class celebrity.

Spending his autumn break at Cape Cod, he'd gone to the bar where he'd accumulated a small audience around him.

A long weekend of peace and quiet is what he'd promised himself but it wasn't going quite to plan. He just couldn't resist being in the limelight.

"Beers all round, "he shouted to the barman. What was he doing, spending money he didn't have?

The word 'twat' ran through his mind, that's exactly what he was but he was unable to control himself.

"Working on it," came the terse response from the barman.

Looking over at the sunlit courtyard beyond the bar

window, he said to hi s small entourage of six, "Why don't we move outside. We'll take the beers out there, mate," he shouted to the barman as he moved towards the exit.

One of the women fluttered her eyelids at Herman, "You must be very rich as well as famous?"

"Oh! I don't talk about my wealth, I try to hide it," he lied, if only she knew the half of it he thought.

She pulled her chair closer towards him and leaned into him, "I can't believe I've e actually met you, can we get a selfie?" she idly stroked a strand of her platinum blonde hair.

In a quick and incomplete thought, he heard himself say, "We can do better than that my dear, how would you like to accompany me for dinner at a great place I've been told about, they've a band playing tonight. I'll get my PA to reserve us a table?"

Back in his suite, which he'd booked at great expense, again at a price he could ill afford, he hastily made the reservation for dinner; there was certainly no PA to do this for him. He arranged for a chauffeur drive to collect his new date Esme and himself at 8pm, having informed her to be ready and waiting in reception.

Herman greeted her in reception, kissing her on the cheek, "Wow! You look amazing! I'm one lucky man to taking you out for dinner."

He loved the way she looked at him, her face agog with awe, as if she'd won first prize on the lottery. His ego shifted up another notch, if she wanted to believe he was a huge celebrity then he'd let her believe it. It could do no harm could it?

Confidently he walked her on his arm to the car where the chauffeur was waiting with the rear doors open for them to enter.

En route Herman held Esme's hand and said, "It's a beautiful restaurant I'm taking you to, one of the best, Michelin-starred. The president has even been known to dine there."

On arrival, they were shown to the dining room with sparkling chandeliers, towering marble columns and soaring floor to ceiling windows overlooking parkland. Studying the menu, he chose the beef and chose the lamb for Esme. He wasn't going to allow her to choose, she might have chosen the lobster, the price of which had caused his eyes to water. The entertainment started, and indeed as he'd expected the band were good.

The service was amicable, the ambience was charming and although the prices were hugely steep, Herman began to relax and enjoy himself.

Esme was glowing and he found her company surprisingly fun and entertaining. The conversation flowed easily as did the red wine he'd ordered and before he knew it she was in his arms on the dance floor. Prior to this date, he'd never thought about love or affection, he'd purely used women for sex. Tonight and Esme were different; he was experiencing a real feeling of affection for her, could it even be love?

Herman had always managed to not allow his emotions to become entangled with women, but he seemed to have lost all power to not become involved emotionally with this one.

As they took their seats back at the table a lady approached them, "Sorry to interrupt you, but aren't you the guy who played Uncle Emil in The Five Sisters? Shame you've not been in anything since then, or have I missed you in something else?"

He liked Esme, and now this stupid woman was going to mess it all up for him.

"Yeah! That's me," he shrugged returning his attention to Esme and his red wine, "Now, if you'll excuse us, we'd like some privacy."

Relief overcame him as the waiter approached, "Would you like to see the desert menu?" He may just have got away with it.

The connection he's made with Esme was strange to him, but he did not doubt the connection in anyway.

He ran his hand through his thick black hair, "Esme, I've not been entirely truthful with you. I'm not a huge celebrity and I don't have a lot of money, I just like to try and impress people. I'm a bit actor who played Uncle Emil in three episodes of The Five Sisters. I've not landed a role in anything since then. I'm sorry, I've tried to be who I'm not."

She smiled at him, "I don't care, I like you, you're good fun and I have more than enough wealth of my own to provide us both with this lifestyle, should things work out between us."

JAMS Publishing

Assignment Forty Nine – We went as far as the car could take us

27th November 2020

J.M. based her story on true events when she was in Barbados during the COVID-19 outbreak, and she did find a haul of drugs on the beach.

Michael delved into an uncomfortable topic, highlighting the lengths that boys will go to escape abuse. Some readers may find the context of this story upsetting.

S.J. enjoyed writing her piece, again exploring romance with a diverse cultural theme. S.J. entered this piece in a Reedsy competition where it reached the final twenty.

Washed Up

By

J. M. McKenzie

Liz and Dave find an unusual package on the beach on their early morning walk. Eli loses something important with devastating consequences.

We went as far as the car could take us. We parked up in the shade, at the point where the pines ended, and the sand began. It was a beautiful day, just like the day before had been, and the day after would be. The cornflower blue sky was streaked with just enough cloud to tame the ferocious heat of the Caribbean sun. A stiff Atlantic breeze swept the white caps onto the golden sand, their final destination after their 4000-mile journey from Senegal.

It was early morning. The beach was empty, but we were not alone. Another car was parked further back in the trees, its darkened windows concealing any occupants. Crabs scuttling from their hidey holes in the sand, stopped to watch as we picked our way down to the water. A trio of Sandpipers chased each receding wave in search of breakfast, nimbly retreating when the next one broke. We had to talk loudly, within earshot of each other, to be heard above the rumbling surf and rattling palm fronds.

Dave fiddled about with his Apple Watch. I gazed out to sea, savouring the warmth of the sun on my face, and drawing in deep slow lungsful of fresh sea air.

"Right! Go!" Dave barked and we set off as briskly as we could. I knew he was keen to beat our fastest time of 43 minutes for 4 laps, end to end. I also knew that the day we had done that, it had been low tide, so we had been walking on the firmest and flattest part of the beach.

Today though, the tide was in. It was going to be a more strenuous, and therefore much slower, walk. Every step was laboured as our feet sank deep into the powder soft sand, and the uneven camber tested our strength and flexibility. Every now and then, an especially large wave would force us to stop and wait till it had passed, or risk being toppled if it caught us mid-step and off balance. Dave strode ahead. I wondered if he would think it was cheating when I followed in his footsteps, where his feet had already flattened and firmed the sand for me.

We were approaching the south end of the beach when we first saw the package. It stood out from among the usual flotsam and jetsam, because of its regular shape. A neat rectangle wrapped in a white nylon sack, about the size of a small suitcase. Dave reached it first.

"What is it?" I asked as I caught up with him. He was fiddling with a yellow cord that tied the sack shut. There was blue writing on the front.

"*Produce of Jamaica. Do not hook.*" I read.

"It's someone's parcels!" Dave exclaimed, as he held up a rectangular object tightly bound in black plastic and parcel tape.

I knew instantly what it was. What *they* were. There were probably 10 or 12 identical parcels inside the sack.

I'd seen Ozark. I'd seen Narcos.

"Dave! It's ... *drugs*! Let's go."

Dave grinned and started trying to open the package.

"Seriously! Put it back!"

I looked up and down the beach. Still empty.

I looked up at the cliffs above. A couple of large houses faced over the beach. Their doors and windows like the features of stern faces staring down at us. Who knew who could be watching us? Was that flash the glint of a binocular lens? Or, worse still, the sight of a sniper rifle. *Stop it! Pull yourself together!*

Dave hauled the sack a bit higher up the beach onto dry sand away from the surf.

"Calm down, Liz. No-one's watching us. Besides, we haven't don't anything wrong."

"I know. But it's just ... I don't know ... a bit *scary*."

Dave laughed. "It's ok, silly." He took my hand. "I'll protect you. You've watched too many movies."

We started walking again.

A few metres further up we found the rest. This time they were light, vacuum packed transparent bags of a brown substance.

"Weed. Jesus!" Dave picked up one of the bags.

"Shit, Dave! I *really* want to go now! I don't like this."

"Someone must have tossed them. Maybe the coastguard was onto them." He looked out to sea.

"Or maybe someone's coming to pick them up. Maybe it's a drop-off."

"Hmm … unlikely."

"Anyway, it doesn't matter. Let's just get out of here. We can call the police when we get back home."

Like the sack, Dave tossed the bags onto the dry sand and we headed back to the car.

There was still no one around except the car with the blacked-out windows.

When we got home, he called the police, referring to himself as a "concerned citizen", and reported that we had found some *unusual* packages on the beach.

***

Eli was nervous. He'd been awake most of the night. He was worried he'd oversleep. He had to be there at dawn for the pick-up and it would take him about an hour to get there.

The bedroom was dark and cool. The mosquito net over the bed, rippled in the soft breeze from the whirring ceiling fan. Myra slept soundly beside him, snoring softly. She smelt of coconut and lavender. She had no idea what he was about to do. Since he'd lost his job at the hotel due to the pandemic, she'd been frantic with worry about how they were going to cope. This was the first time in weeks that she'd slept properly herself. He'd told her it was a fishing a job. A friend of a friend and all that. She'd bought it completely.

He hated lying to her, but she'd never have let him go through with it. But it was too good an opportunity to miss. It all seemed so easy. So straightforward. Be at the beach at first light. Pick up the merchandise and deliver it to an address on the other side of the island before midday. Three thousand dollars cash on delivery. No questions asked.

He'd planned to get up at 4.30 and leave at 5, but in the end, when it was clear that sleep was going to elude him, he got up and left at 3. Better to be there early anyway. Just in case. Myra never stirred. He kissed her forehead gently before he slipped away.

He reached the beach around 4am and parked under the trees.

He settled down to wait for dawn.

***

Eli woke to sound of a car pulling up.

Shit! It was light! He looked at his watch. 6.30! He'd missed the pick-up time! *Oh, sweet Jesus!*

The car parked a few metres away and a man and a woman got out. Tourists. Dressed for exercise. Tight nylon vests and shorts. Sunglasses. The man wore a tattered baseball cap and the woman a bright pink headband that pulled her long dark hair off her face. The woman glanced over at his car. Even though he knew she couldn't see him through the tinted glass, he slumped down in his seat.

Oh, please God, make them go away.

They didn't. The woman walked down to the sea. The man fiddled with his watch. After a few seconds he called to her and she followed as he started to stride down the beach.

Eli was beside himself. He punched the dashboard.

Shit! Shit! Shit! How could he have a been so stupid? He opened the car door and then shut it again. He couldn't let them see him. But he had to see if it was there. Had to see what they would do if they found it. *Oh God.* If they found it! He was a dead man! *Calm down! Calm Down! Wait a few minutes then get out and watch the from the cover of the trees.*

A couple of minutes felt like a lifetime, but he forced himself to wait, even timing himself on his watch. After three minutes exactly, he got out and scurried over to where the trees were thicker. He edged closer to the beach.

They were already half way along. He franticly scoured the waterline ahead of them for his drop-off. A flash of white stood out against the pale gold of the sand. There it was. The sack. *Oh, dear god!* They were heading straight for it!

The man stopped and pointed at the sack before walking over to it. He bent over and seemed to be trying to open it. Eli felt sick. *No! No! No! Leave it alone you fool!* The woman caught up with him. The man took a package out of the sack. He straightened up and turned it over in his hands, examining it. Eli closed his eyes and ran his hands through his hair. *Don't panic! Don't panic. Just see what they do next! It might still be ok.* Who was he kidding?

He opened his eyes again to see the woman walking quickly away. *Sensible.* But the man was hauling the sack up the beach. *Idiot!* But then he left the sack where it was and followed the woman. *Good man. Good man. Keep going. Keep going.*

He continued to watch as they carried on towards the

end of the beach. They stopped a couple more times to look at other items on the sand that he couldn't make out from where he was. Then suddenly, they turned and headed back. This time they passed the sack without touching it or even going near it. Eli sank to his knees. He was almost weeping. *Thank you, God,! Thank you, Jesus,!*

He waited for them to leave.

***

Eli was almost back at the car when he heard the sirens. The sack was heavy, and the other packages had been scattered over the beach. It had taken him too long to gather them all up and start to move them. And it was getting late. Other people had started arriving, so he'd had to retreat back to the trees. He made slow progress, picking his way among the roots and fallen branches.

Two police 4x4 vehicles sped down the access road to the parking area. Their blue lights were flashing.

Eli dropped the sack and ran.

***

Article from The Herald, The Newspaper of St Lucia

Monday, October 26, 2020

Local chef, Eli Payne, 29, who lost his job when the Sandals resort closed due to the pandemic, was found dead yesterday in Parish Lands. Police say the cause of death was multiple gunshot wounds. Police suspect another drug-related killing. Eli's wife, Myra Payne, 27, said she has no idea what he was doing in Parish Lands. She believed him to be on a fishing trip on the other side of the island.

Escape
By
Michael Andrews

A car is a vehicle for many uses. To explore new places, to get to work or to school. For the young brothers Luke and Max, it is a vehicle of escape. However, not all escape routes lead to a place of haven.

We went as far as the car would take us. I could hear the spluttering of the engine over the radio and the car lurched beneath us as it finally ran out of gas. I turned the wheel and steered the slowing car to the side of the road, frustration and anger beginning to boil up inside me. I stretched my leg so that my foot could reach the brake and the car pulled to a stop. I leaned forward and turned off the radio and took in deep breaths to try to calm myself.

Silent darkness surrounded us. The occasional hoot of an owl was the only noise that I could hear through the gap in the window by my side. Then, a slight wind started to blow and the branches of the trees that lined the road conducted their own orchestra of creaks and cracks.

I glanced over to the passenger seat where Max, my eight-year-old brother, was fast asleep. I could hear a soft snuffle as he breathed in through his nose and out through his mouth. I reached over to brush the blonde lock of hair that had fallen over his closed eyes and the anger began to boil inside me once again.

Instead of the perfectly tanned skin of the playful, sport loving boy was the growing purple and black bruise where HE had hit him. I pulled my handkerchief from my pocket and dabbed at the cut on his lip, the white cotton turning red with his blood.

His blanket had slipped slightly so I pulled it back up, tucking it underneath his chin and kissed him softly on the forehead. He was my world. He was my brother, and I would do anything to protect him.

Opening the car door quietly so as not to wake Max, I eased myself from my seat. My aching and bruised muscles screamed at me and as I bit back the gasp of pain that was threatening to escape my lips, I turned back to look over Max and was pleased to see that he was still asleep.

"I swore to you that I'd protect him, Mum," I muttered, the words spilling shakily from my mouth. I slumped down on the muddy ground, my back leaning against the cold metal of the door of the car. I felt the tears begin to leak from my eyes and my body shook as the adrenaline left my body. Curling into a ball, I bit my right fist to stifle the sobs and I cried.

I cried for my dead mother, passed some six months. I cried for the bruises on my body, the welts from my father's belt, the aches where my ribs were still cracked from the punches from his fists, the lump on the back of my head where I had fallen against the bedside cabinet. I shouldn't have to have this responsibility at my age, I was only twelve, but I would look after my younger brother with my last breath.

"No more!" I sniffled, wiping my nose. "Gotta be strong for Max." Forcing myself up from the wet mud, I opened the back door to the car where I had pushed the two hastily packed backpacks. Feeling underneath them, I found the bottle of juice that I had filled. Whilst I was taking a long gulp from the bottle, I heard a whimper from the front of the car.

"Luke?" Max's voice had a hint of panic in it and I heard limbs flailing.

"I'm here, Max!" I said loudly, moving back and sitting in the driver's seat once again. Handing the juice bottle to Max, I stroked his face and head before pulling him into a hug. He squirmed over the gear stick until he was in my lap.

"I'm sorry..." he started to sob.

"Don't you dare," I said, a little harsher than I meant to. I felt his body stiffen in my arms, so I kissed the top of his head and held him until he settled down.

"What time is it? Where are we? What are we going to do?" His voice sounded so afraid, so young. I needed to be in charge, to be confident even though I was shitting myself as well.

"It's a little after ten. I don't know where we are," I admitted hugging him tightly to reassure him. "We're about two hundred miles away but we've run out of gas."

"WHAT?" he shouted and panicked in my arms. "What are we going to do? How are we going to get more?"

"We're not," I sighed. "Look, let's get some sleep and we can think about what we are going to do in the morning. Why don't you scoot over onto the back seat so you can lay down properly?"

We moved the bags into the boot of the car and Max lay down under his blanket. I made sure that both the back doors were locked before getting into the passenger seat and tilting it back slightly so that I could get some sleep of my own.

Sleep was a long time coming.

***

I was late getting home from school. I swore at myself for being stupid enough for stepping in between Billy Jacobs and the Harris twins, but I couldn't let little Billy get beaten up by those bullies one more time. Unfortunately, Mr Larson had come around the corner just as I punched Freddie and I was the one who ended up in after school detention.

I crashed through the back door, my breath coming in short, ragged pants as I tried to recover from my mile and a half sprint from school. I hated not being there when Dad got home from work. I normally had enough time to prepare dinner and have a cold bottle of beer waiting for him as he walked through the door.

"Dad! I'm sorry I'm late," I half yelled, but he wasn't in the kitchen or the lounge. I stopped in my tracks, holding my breath. Maybe he had gone to the bar after getting home. Maybe my luck had held.

Then I heard the cries coming from Max's room and the sound of leather hitting flesh.

I opened the door to Max's room. My eight-year-old brother was bent over his desk, shorts down by his ankles with my father stood behind him. He had his belt in his hand, raised above his head and as I watched, he lashed it downwards against my brother's bare buttocks. Then I saw my father drop his own jeans and underwear and leaned over my brother.

I froze.

No, not Max. He couldn't do it to Max. That's what I was there for. He told me I was taking Mum's place and that Max would be left alone as long as I didn't make a fuss. As long as I behaved.

For six months I had behaved. For six months I let Dad do stuff to me, with me.

Max's scream pierced my brain.

My mind went blank. I don't even recall having gone to the kitchen to get the knife.

I barely remember grabbing Max, pulling on his clothes and getting into Dad's car.

***

I awoke suddenly, sweat pouring from my body. Max was screaming and I scrambled over the seat into the back of the car. I cradled Max into my arms and held him until his cries settled into gentle sobs. I felt him press against me and his lips pressed against mine.

"I'll be your boy," Max whispered softly. "I promise."

For a moment, I didn't know what to do, what was happening. I felt his soft lips and I felt love. We wrapped our arms around each other, and I felt peace. Then his words echoed in my mind.

"No!" I said, pulling away from Max. "I'm not Dad, I'm not like that."

Max started to cry, and I pulled him back to me. Holding him against me, I kissed his head and his cheek, but once he had calmed down, I turned his face towards me.

"Listen Max, what Dad did was wrong," I said. "I tried to not let him do it to you, but I failed. I'm so sorry."

"I know you are," Max sighed softly. "I know about sex stuff, and I thought that I could stop him from hurting you if I let him do it to me."

I cried.

My little brother knew what HE had been doing. I held Max as I sobbed. Six months of pain flowed from me and I found my brother, my Max, holding me, comforting me.

I looked at him through tear stained eyes. His own blue eyes, bright with tears, shone back at me.

"We beat him though, didn't we?"

I laughed, snorted really. I wiped the snot from my nose.

"Yeah, we fucking did," I said. I pulled Max to me. "I promised Mum I'd look after you and I will. I promise."

"I love you, Luke," Max said and hugged me once more. He snuggled down, placing his head underneath my chin.

Sleep came quickly.

***

I felt safe, I felt warmth. I awoke in the arms of my brother. I glanced upwards and saw Luke sleeping. My older brother was my hero. He'd protected me ever since my mother had died. My Dad was a bastard. He was a pervert.

Neither of them knew it but I had seen Dad going into Luke's room at night. I didn't know what they were doing at first, but I soon figured out that Dad was doing sex stuff with Luke. I thought that it was wrong; boys don't do sex stuff with each other... especially dads and sons but Luke seemed to like it.

So, I never said anything. As long as Luke liked it, I guessed it was okay.

I tried to ask Luke about it, about sex, but he never wanted to talk about it. I guess he didn't like me like that. Dad liked him, not me. I guess Luke liked Dad like that too.

I tried to make Luke like me, but he just told me to go to my room whenever Dad and him wanted to have their fun. I hated not being involved. I just wanted Luke to love me like he loved Dad.

Then today, Luke was late home, and I got the chance to tell Dad that I wanted to be his boy just like Luke. It was a mistake. He hurt me. I don't know why Luke liked it, why he begged Dad to take him to his bedroom and not me, but I'm glad he did.

Dad slapped me across the face really hard before dragging me into my bedroom. Dad pulled my shorts and underwear down and hit me with his belt. It really hurt and I was crying. I felt Dad put his hands on my hips. I'm sure that I heard Luke shouting. Dad pulled away and I was left alone. I was alone. I turned to see Luke and my

Dad embrace and then Dad fell to the floor. Luke was holding a knife and had a weird look on his face. He leaned down over Dad's body with the knife.

***

Blue lights were flashing. I wiped my eyes and hugged Max towards me. He was awake. His eyes were pools of beauty and I felt love, so much love. I hugged him and he hugged me back. I squirmed and shifted around, my boxer shorts riding up. Max had a smile on his face.

"I love you, Luke," he said softly and kissed me on the cheek.

I shook my head.

There was a knock on the window.

I looked up and there were two policemen staring in, torches shining through the window. I unlocked the door and I stared at them as they opened it.

"Luke Meadows?"

"Yes," I replied.

"I am arresting you on suspicion of the murder of Harrison Meadows," the officer said as he pulled me out of the car. I tried to hide my near naked body and he had the decency to let me grab the blanket.

"But I didn't..." I started to lie *'How had they found us already?'*.

"Your father has been found mutilated, his genitals cut off, and his throat cut. You're here two hundred miles away from home in his car." The officer looked at me. "Son, you need to come up with some sort of story to keep you off the electric chair. People round here don't like boys who kill their pops."

I felt warm liquid trickle down my leg as I collapsed onto the ground. I was pulled back to my feet.

"Sir," Max said politely as he climbed out of the back seat.

He held a cloth-wrapped package in his hands. He unwrapped it and a bloody kitchen knife fell to the ground.

"Luke didn't do nothing sir," Max said. "Daddy hurt both of us, so I made him stop."

"No Max," I started.

I watched as he picked up the knife and started towards the policeman holding me.

"Let him go or I will hurt you as well," Max hissed.

"Put the knife down, son," the officer said, his hand unbuckling the clip on his gun holster.

"I'M NOT YOUR SON!" Max shouted and ran at him.

The sound of a firecracker echoed in my eyes. I watched as a patch of red started to grow on the front of Max's white t-shirt. Max's eyes had opened wide with shock and a gasp of pain escaped his mouth as he dropped to his knees.

A hysterical wail echoed in my ears and it took a moment to realise that it had come from my mouth. Pain erupted in my chest as my brother fell forward, face down into a dirty puddle of mud. I ran to him, dropping onto my knees and hugged his lifeless body to mine.

Despite my pleas to God, the Devil and anyone else that was listening, two pools of dead eyes stared back into my own tear-filled eyes. A flash of light caught my attention, and I spotted the knife, dropped by Max, lying in the mud next to me.

Grimly, I picked it up and stood, turning towards the murderer of my brother.

"I'll fucking kill you."

I ran towards him.

Firecrackers popped once more, and I was thrown backwards.

Laying in the mud, my head was turned towards my Dad's car. I had hoped that the car would take us to a new start, a new home. In a way it had. It had taken us somewhere else. It had taken us to Hell.

I'm Different From Other Girls
by
S.J. Gibbs

We are in the densest of jungles, yet another adventure. Who do we meet? Are we in danger? Can love be found where you least expect to find it?

We went as far as the car would take us.

We are in the densest of jungles, no other humans around.

There is no alternative route, the only way through now, is by foot.

This is by no means the first adventure, my mother and myself had encountered. Since my birth, sixteen years ago, we have never settled anywhere for longer than three months.

My mother's knowledge of the jungle is impressive, but then most of whatever she decides for us to do, is the same. Most of her skills, she'd learned from my Grandfather, God bless his soul, and the life she'd lived with him is now being passed down to me. I've never known my father.

I follow her at a pace, her long, muscular legs drawing my eyes.

It is a misty and overcast morning, and despite our waterproofs and strong hiking boots, it's not long, before I feel slightly soggy.

The clouds thicken and gather and drops of rain begin to fall on us.

I concentrate, I follow, rest will come just hours away.

My mother notices every nuance of the jungle, and I have learned to do the same.

I'm different from other girls, I've seen plenty of them, all over the world, but I've never met one that's travelled the way we have. Sure, I've met a few who have been travelling for two or three years, but they all settle somewhere eventually, just not us. My mother strides on.

She asks for nothing else from me except a determination to keep up with her.

If this displeases me in any way, then she says it is only because I have a limited understanding of what is good for me.

I spot them first, but it's only a split second before mother sees them, three tribesmen standing before us, staring at us, motionless, glaring with evil eyes at us intruders who have so suddenly appeared in their land.

I feel the need for air in my throat, and I clear my throat hoarsely.

Heaviness settles into the pit of my stomach; even though I know my mother will find a way of making their wildly divergent understandings of who we are and what we want, fade away.

They look at my mother and then at myself, a penetrating stare, which goes right through me. As I've been taught, I stand motionless, and try not to draw any attention to myself.

One of them snarls, a deep guttural, inhuman sound.

He appears agitated, but I don't think he means to harm us.

I watch as my mother lowers her head as an act of respect, offers her hand to the one that has snarled, and says, "I'm not your enemy."

She gestures to me, and I move towards her as she gently tucks me into the crook of her arm. I lower my head in respect to the tribesmen.

Their eyes and hair are wild, but their response is mild-mannered. My mother has taught me that more often than not, most tribe's people, especially those who have never encountered a white person, are highly superstitious, of harming another human unless they are a known enemy, for fear of retribution by whatever gods or spiritual beliefs their particular tribe holds.

My mothers actions seem to be effective again, we appear to be at peace with one another, as they lead us even further into the jungle.

Mosquitoes and biting gnats nibble at my face, reminding me how grateful I am that the rest of my body is covered by my waterproofs. The men leading us are not afforded such a luxury, but seem unperturbed, as if they don't even exist.

After wandering for many hours, we finally enter a clearing.

This was the moment, which always took the most courage, to keep my feelings and emotions at bay, whilst the rest of the tribe and the chief overlook us and decide whether we are to be welcomed.

We are presented to the chief at the opening of his hut.

By now, I am exhausted but my mother has taught me never to show weakness, not even when you feel as though you are unable to take one more step, or even when it is a sheer effort to hold up your own head.

A young girl, about my age, possibly a little younger stands to the chief's side. I am uncertain as to whether she is his daughter, or his wife.

The chief looks us over; we bend our heads to show respect. He reaches for a horn and blows into it. I dare to look up, have we been accepted? It appears we have, as tribes people circle around us. At first, staring at us with looks of disbelief, and then dancing and chanting begins. It is clearly a ceremony of initiation, establishing an alliance between us, offering us a bond of kinship.

One of the tribesmen takes me by the hand and leads me into a circle, made-up of others. He gyrates in front of me, and dances around me. Although a little fearful, I smile in response.

A beautiful lady with thick, dark hair down to her waist enters the circle and stands beside me. With such little clothing, her advanced pregnancy is blatant. She holds my hand and moves it to her bare stomach. I feel the unborn child kick. Tears fill my eyes at such total acceptance.

The feral look on her face is at one with my own, after all I am feral, I've been raised feral.

I follow her to her own hut, and I sit with her.

Human emotion is complex, but with her and this tribe I now feel at peace.

I help her to wash out her pots and pans.

Her soft forehead is moist with sweat.

A red dragonfly zooms around my head, and I watch as it settles on a leaf.

A young tribesman approaches and sits by my side. An older man stands behind him; I assume it's their father.

I smile at the boy; he looks about the same age as me.

He smiles back. I pause, an unfamiliar sensation makes my blood quicken and electricity bolts through me, making my skin tingle.

He scoops up a handful of dirt and places it in front of me.

This action intensifies my spirit.

My eyes move to the angry clouds above.

I look back at him, he's very handsome, he's probably a head and shoulders taller than me, and twice as broad. The expression on my face is reflected on his.

How can this be happening? How can I be falling in love with this boy, who I've only just met?

I sigh, my attention still on him, unable to move my focus.

A rip of thunder causes me to startle.

My questions of common sense are rendered ineffective.

I'm confused, as everything seems to be happening so fast, I've never responded to a boy this way before.

His hand moves to mine, and as we touch I am fully part of him, my soul is complete.

I look around for my mother, but she has gone inside the hut with the chief. Would she object? Would the chief object?

Although we don't speak the same language, something I've experienced many times before, our eyes and body language are communicating.

A man younger than the father, but older than the boy enters and sits down next to the pregnant lady. I soon establish it's the boy's older brother, the husband of the pregnant lady.

I'm at home here, at one with nature, I've never liked the towns or cities we've visited.

I don't feel as though this is my first time here, I feel as though this is where I belong.

I gaze at the boy again, and my heart flutters.

The pregnant woman serves dinner, encouraged by the boy, I dive in, I'm starving.

After we've eaten, I help to clear and wash the pans. The boy takes my hand and leads me to his place of sleep. We sit down and he touches my soft face. I'm not sure what to do or think about, but I'm enamoured of this boy, whose name I have now established is Ibrahima. It's almost as if I'm living in some type of fairy-tale.

I don't know why but I always thought I'd fall in love with a white man, but here I am in the middle of the jungle with a tribesman, and I already know for sure that I'm in love.

I don't understand what he says to me, but his voice, soothes and calms me.

Mosquitoes buzz around us, but they no longer bother me the way they had before.

I'd removed my waterproofs earlier and now I remove my jeans and my man's dress shirt, and I reveal myself in my underwear.

I glance at him to see him watching me. Ibrahima gestures to me with his hand.

I lean into him, at peace yet hyped up on adrenaline and desire.

Innocence leaves me, "Oh God," I cry softly.

His expertise, surprises me.

It is an amazing night; I have never been made to feel so beautiful.

The dawn light enters his hut, and he slings one of his long legs over me.

My mother enters the hut, expressing her dissatisfaction with what she sees before her. It is now an unpleasant situation.

A young woman of the tribe stands beside her.

"He has been unfaithful to this young lady, he is promised to her. What have you done, you stupid girl," my mother shouts.

My eyes dash to the young woman, then to Ibrahima, then back to my mother. I feel betrayed.

"Why didn't you check up on me last night and protect me?" I shout back at my mother.

Her eyes fill with terror, "Because I thought you knew better. I trusted you. You're no longer a baby, you're sixteen."

My fairy-tale was quickly turning into a grim realistic story.

"Thanks for the information," I snap at her.

I look at Ibrahima, his face is gloomy and his lips compressed.

My face colours, at the memory of the lovemaking, which had lasted for hours.

A silence fell over the hut.

I watch as the young woman slips a ring from her finger and hands it to me.

"Well, there you go," my mother, says, "He doesn't need two wives does he?"

I want to leave the hut, but something stops me from doing so.

Whilst my state of undress is hardly more modest than the young woman's, I grab my underwear, jeans and shirt and rapidly get dresses.

As I do so, I glare into Ibrahima's almond shaped eyes, the brown of his irises so dark that they are almost black, "Somebody screwed up, I guess," I say to him.

The sound of steps approach the hut, and the chief enters.

Immediately, he dismisses the young woman.

He takes the ring from my hand, and offers it to Ibrahima. Words are exchanged between them and then the chief indicates to me to come over. Ibrahima looks into my eyes with such love, my heart pounds, and he places the ring on my finger.

My mother speaks, "That's it, you're promised to him now. Do you realise what you've done?"

I didn't know who to be most annoyed with, my mother or Ibrahima, but one thing I knew for sure was the fact I was promised to him gave me a warm glow, deep within my heart.

I gasped, and then realised the sound had come from my own throat.

I'm not leaving with you this time, when you move on," I heard myself say.

By the end of the following day, after many discussions and the fact she had witnessed Ibrahima and the way he was with me, my mother had adapted and was more at ease with the idea of me staying with him, when she decided to move on.

Her conception of life, never to settle in one place, was now hers and no longer mine. Every day Ibrahima showed me more marvellous and exceptional qualities. I was well and truly in love.

JAMS Publishing

Assignment Fifty - Darryl slid three quarters into the vending machine and weighed his options

22nd January 2021

J.M. had some fun with this piece, experimenting with a flashback storyline with a dark twist.

Michael chose to write a topical piece inspired by the events surrounding the death of George Floyd.

S.J. turned her hand to a crime story, but agreed that it wasn't one of her better pieces.

M&M Memories
By
J.M. McKenzie

Darryl can't remember anything about his past - and doesn't want to.

Darryl slid three quarters into the vending machine and weighed his options. The candy occupied the fourth and fifth rows, between the savory snacks and the Grandmas Cookies. It struck him that, considering this was a hospital, there was a distinct lack of healthy choices available. It also struck him that, despite not knowing who he was or where he was from, he knew how to operate a vending machine. And, although he didn't know his own name (Darryl was the name the nurses had given him because he reminded them of the Darryl character in the Team Thor movies), he knew the names of all the candy bars.

Another thing he did know, was that he wasn't in search of a healthy snack. He had been craving the rich and heady combination of sweet, creamy, milk chocolate and soft caramel for days. As soon as he'd been allowed out of bed, he'd wheeled his IV stand down the corridor to the elevator lobby, in search of his sugar fix. Now, he was torn between the chewy nougat, and the promise of a peanut of two, in the Snickers bar, and the crisp snap of the finger biscuits in the Twix. *Twix or Snickers? Snickers or Twix? 42 or 46? 46 or 42?* He couldn't decide.

A small, but restless, queue was forming behind him. Beads of sweat broke out on his forehead. His palms were slick with moisture. He wiped them on the front of his hospital gown. *Twix! No, Snickers! No, Twix. No! It had to be Snickers!* He punched in the number. Four ... His finger hovered over the six. But his gaze drifted to the seven. His finger followed. What was wrong with him? *Push the six! Get the Snickers. SIX! SIX! SIX!*

He pushed the seven.

"Shit!" He punched the six. Jabbed it again and again! Hammered it furiously in a sudden frenzy of rage as the bright yellow packet of M&M's began to move jerkily towards the front.

"Damn it!" he yelled as the packet dropped into the tray with a soft rattle. He slammed his palm against the glass. The machine shuddered.

"Hey, Buddy! Are you ok?" the man behind him asked.

"OF COURSE, IM NOT OK! DO I LOOK LIKE I'M OK? I *WANTED* THE SNICKERS!"

The man's mouth dropped open. He looked as if he was going to speak then appeared to think better of it. Instead, he cleared his throat and shuffled back a couple of paces, examining his finger nails. Darryl turned and headed back down the corridor. He'd had to borrow the 95 cents from the guy in the next room. He wasn't going to be defeated. He had to get more money.

"Hey!" the man shouted after him. "You forgot your candy!"

Darryl turned, about to unleash a torrent of abuse. The man was waving the yellow packet of M&M's at him.

Then the flashback hit.

It wasn't the first one. That had happened the day he'd woken up. They had just taken out his breathing tube and helped him to sit up and take a few sips of iced water through a straw. He had no idea where he was, or how he'd got there. Couldn't remember a thing. His name. Where he lived. What he did. Whether he was married or had a family. Nothing. His mind was just one big black hole. They were telling him not to worry. That he'd had a nasty bang on the head. That it was normal at this stage. That it would all come back in time.

Then, one of the nurses smoothed the bedspread over his body. His eyes were drawn to her hands. They were small and soft and pink, against the blue woven fabric. Her nails were short and clean. The hands looked familiar. Like some he'd seen before. Somewhere ... else.

The colours around the edges of his vision began to blur and distort. It was as if he was looking down a watery tunnel. At the end of the tunnel, caught in a circle of light, the nurse's hands moved quietly. Every detail of them was bright and intense. Every skin crease, every tiny golden hair, every blemish, was illuminated and magnified. Then, the blue of the bedspread faded to a dull grey. Its uniform, linear surface became rough and uneven. The hands stopped moving and lay, palms up, pale and still. The warm pink nailbeds faded to a cold blue, and the skin took on a waxy, sallow appearance.

Darryl realised it was a memory pushing through. If he let it, he knew the picture would widen and he would see who the hands belonged to. But he didn't want to. A deep, dark dread washed over him. His skin crawled and his gut clenched. He closed his eyes and pushed back against the pillows, away from the image.

"No. No! NO!" he screamed.

"Darryl! Darryl!" The nurse with the small hands was touching his cheek. Gently.

He opened his eyes.

"It's alright Darryl. You're safe. We've got you. Don't worry. It'll all come back. It'll all come back with time."

But Darryl didn't want it to come back. From that moment, Darryl took great comfort in not knowing who he was, where he had come from and … what he had done. He didn't want it all to come back with time. He didn't want it to come back at all.

After that were others. One or two a day. All the same. All triggered by a simple sight, sound or smell. A glossy, swinging, auburn ponytail, a peal of girlish laughter, a waft of familiar perfume. Each one would send him spiralling back down the watery tunnel. Each time, more details were revealed. A once swinging auburn ponytail, now limp and still. A once laughing mouth, now silent, its blue lips parted and breathless. A once fresh and vibrant perfume, now stale and faded under the scent of death and decay. It was as if he was completing a terrible jigsaw puzzle, piece by piece.

Other things were happening too. The nurses spent less and less time with him. Their warm and friendly smiles and touches replaced by wary expressions and minimal physical contact. Men in suits came to talk to him, asking him questions about what he could remember (which of course was nothing). Over the past couple of days, a uniformed police officer had been stationed at either end of the corridor. He didn't know if they were there for him. Until today he'd been confined to bed. Nevertheless, he'd waited for the one near the vending machine to go to the bathroom before he had left his room.

And now it was the M&M's at the end of the tunnel. Small hands with short clean fingernails picking them out of the packet one by one. Popping them between smiling pink lips. The bobbing ponytail. The laughter. The perfume.

Then, the M&M packet was lying on the rough, uneven surface. Its contents rolled across the floor. Blue, yellow, green … red. Red on red. Red smears on the pale, cold hands. Wet, red strands in the limp, auburn pony tail. Frothy red bubbles between the blue parted lips.

Darryl closed his eyes. He shut out the image. He turned away.

When he opened them again, one of the police officers was walking down the corridor towards him. A hand gripped his shoulder firmly from behind.

"I think you'd better come back to your room now, Sir. We have a few more questions we'd like to ask you."

Life's Battles
By
Michael Andrews

When a hungry homeless man battles a stubborn vending machine, he doesn't realize that the true battle is about to begin.

Darryl slid three quarters into the vending machine and weighed his options. He felt the hunger pangs in his stomach and quickly punched in the three-digit code. The machine whirred and he scratched his stubbled chin as the spiral metal holder twisted itself to release its bounty of food.

"Oh, fucks sake!" Darryl hissed as he saw the chip packet snag on the final arm of the holder. Glancing up and down the street, he braced his shoulder against the machine and rocked it gently. He could almost hear the machine's condescending laughter as the packet swayed for a moment before settling back onto its precarious perch.

"Goddammit!" He leaned back before barging the machine. Again, the chip packet mocked him by attempting to fall but decided to stay in place. He stood back and saw his reflection in the glass of the vending machine, and his heart sank a little more than normal. Long gone were the once bright eyes of his youth with dark brown orbs of sadness staring back. His cheeks were shallow, gaunt-like, and his greasy hair was a tangled mess of knots that was in desperate need of a wash.

"Fucking smelly nigga!"

He frowned at the snide comments of a group of teenage schoolboys as they walked past him, and the stench of his unwashed body sneaked past the mental block of his condition. He gagged slightly before his stomach rumbled once again, reminding him of his hunger. He dropped his shoulder and charged at the machine.

A resounding crack echoed in his ears before Darryl felt pain in his arm. A trickle ran down his forehead and he felt a sting in his left eye, but he was too focused on his prize. He reached out and grabbed the packet of chips that had been stubbornly refusing to become his. It was then that he saw the shard of glass that had run through his upper arm. He stared at it, detached from reality for a moment as he watched the red stream of blood run down his arm.

"What the bloody hell is going on?" A harsh voice shocked Darryl back into the present.

"The packet got stuck," he blubbed out, the pain suddenly hitting his brain and tears started to leak from his eyes.

"A likely story," the store owner hissed at him as he grabbed the chip packet out of Darryl's weakening grip. Fishing his cell phone from out of his apron, he dialled 9-1-1 and waited for a moment. "Yeah, I need the police to 14 Maine Street," he muttered. "Some dirty homeless negro has broken up my vending machine trying to steal food."

"No sir," Darryl's voice stuttered. "I put my money in, sir, I did."

He tried to reach out to the man but slumped down as his vision started to blur.

"Sir, can you call for an ambulance?" Darryl heard the voice of a woman and felt a compression on his arm. He looked up and saw a boy of around twelve pulling off his school tie. Compassionate blue eyes stared into Darryl's as the boy fashioned a makeshift tourniquet around his arm. The look of worry on the pale face of the schoolboy was comforting... someone cared about him after all.

"Mom, I don't think we should touch the glass." His voice sounded sweet to Darryl's ears.

"Are you an angel?" he asked, his head beginning to get dizzy with the loss of blood.

"No sir. I'm Jayden... I'm going to help you till the medics get here."

In the background, Darryl could hear raised voices as Jayden's mother and the store owner argued back and forth before the sounds of sirens filled the air. A screech of tires was followed by the slamming of car doors.

"Get away from him, boy!" a deep voice shouted.

"No way," Jayden said. "He's bleeding to death and I'm not moving until the ambulance gets here."

A scream pierced Darryl's ear and his hazy vision saw his little angel being man-handled by a uniformed man who looked to be at least two hundred pounds.

"Leave him be!" Darryl gasped out, trying to get up to help the young boy before he was pushed backwards and onto his front. Pain exploded in his head as his arms were twisted behind his back and he felt the cold snap of metal on his wrists.

"Shit, look at this glass shard," another voice said as a second policeman knelt down beside the now stricken Darryl. "Best pull it out."

"NO!" Jayden's shout rang out. "He'll bleed out for sure if you take it out."

"Shut up, boy," the first policeman snapped. "We're in charge here."

Darryl's shriek of pain could be heard from down the street as the jagged piece of glass was roughly pulled from his arm, tearing muscle and sinew. Unable to hold back, Darryl's stomach heaved but with the lack of food, only a stream of acidic tasting bile spewed from his mouth. He started to struggle, knowing that his life was being measured in minutes. He did not want to meet his maker face down on a dirty sidewalk.

"Oh no, you're not going anywhere," one of the policemen laughed harshly and whilst the first held Darryl's body, a second placed his knee on the neck of the struggling captive.

"I can't breathe," Darryl gasped out.

"Let him go!" Jayden's mother was screaming whilst being held back.

"Stay back!" Four further officers had turned up and were wielding their batons in an attempt to hold the growing crowd at bay.

"I... can't... breathe." Darryl's voice was ragged, panicky.

"Leave him alone!" Jayden shouted before his own cry of pain was heard. Darryl saw the boy hit the ground, his eyes closed, a stream of red blood pouring from the gash in his forehead where the baton had struck him.

The crowd erupted angrily at the sight of the young white boy being felled. More sirens and screeching tyres were a fading background noise to Darryl whose vision was tunnelling into blackness.

"I...

"Can't...

"Bree."

"Mom?" Jayden's voice was weak as he shook his head only to regret it instantly. Machines beeped next to him. He looked around and recognised that he was in a hospital room. His clothes were gone, and he was in a blue, paper gown. He blushed for a moment at the thought that someone had undressed him while he had been unconscious. He started to raise his hand to his head, but the clank of metal shocked him. Both of his hands were cuffed to the bed.

"MOM! HELP!"

A door opened and a man stepped inside the room. Instead of the white coat of a doctor, it was the blue uniform of a policeman.

"Well, the little nigger lover is awake," he spat. "Your little scene cost me two of my friends today."

"Wha...?" the boy croaked out.

He watched as the policeman turned on the television in the corner and was shocked to see scenes that belonged in a movie, not real life. Rioting crowds were smashing up cars and shops and running battles with police. A tickertape banner was scrolling across the bottom of the screen. Jayden took a deep breath as he read the news of 12 dead with hundreds injured.

"Before you think that any good will come from this," the cop sneered. "You did nothing. That nigger is dead and, oh, so is your Mom. Maybe look after your own next time."

The man hocked his throat and Jayden flinched as he felt a gob of spittle hit his face just below his eyeline. The cop smiled a sadistic smile and turned away, closing the door behind him as he took his position back outside the boy hero's room.

"Mom... I'm sorry," Jayden whispered and didn't realise that the trickle down his cheeks were his tears and not the spittle from the cop. He closed his eyes, wishing that he was dead. A vision of two people came to him, smiling down and his mother's voice filled his head.

'Don't be sorry, my brave little Angel. Darryl and I are with God now. Be safe and be strong.'

Don't Mess with the Mob
by
S.J.Gibbs

Darryl's court duties are over as foreman of the jury. A new life awaits, but will he ever get to experience it?

Darryl slid three quarters into the vending machine and weighed his options.

His court duties were presumably over now that the case was settled.

He hoped so as his baby was due to be born any day now, and he'd been dreading missing the birth due to his role on the jury.

The case had lasted weeks, a mob killing, which had caused him pain and distress to sit through and debate with the other jurors. The graphic images of the dead body with its long thin, half-severed neck and its face stained with blood and dust were ones he was sure would never leave him.

No wonder he had felt so solemn lately, living in a hotel room, being escorted back and forth to the courtroom daily.

It had caused him great dissatisfaction to be called as a juror in the first place, but to become stuck on such a huge case, had gone beyond anything he could even have imagined.

His mind knew every corner of the courtroom as he'd tried to avert his eyes from the evil ones of the man who'd stood accused of the killing. The patterns in the slabs of the creamy white Istrian stone and the red Verona marble, which gave a delicate rosy-orange hue to the room, far preferable to looking into those eyes, for fear of what they may have signalled back to him.

He wiped his brow, the heat of the court building made him feel as though he'd been sitting in a sauna for hours.

The ringing cell phone from its place in the pocket of his jeans shattered his concentration, but before he answered he selected the button E5, which would deliver him a mini wheat bagel with butter and cream cheese.

The name Trisha flashed across the cell phone screen. The soon-to-be mother of his baby, and most perfect friend n the entire world.

Accepting her call, the contours of her face lit-up his screen.

Her voice was fast and furious, "Darryl, I'm in labour, I'm on the way to the hospital," she almost screamed.

Running to the car park exit of the court building, he shouted back, "I'm on my way, I'll be there as soon as I can."

As he drove at neck-break speed, his despair from being involved on the case changed to new hope for the baby and the life that now lay before them.

The hospital lay in the next valley, only a thirty-minute drive from the courthouse, only thirty minutes before he could be with her. Tricia his first love, his only love, childhood sweethearts since they had been sixteen, and now fourteen years later, their first baby was about to be born.

The journey although a short one, seemed to stretch for a thousand miles.

Darryl hoped he had plenty of time; he reassured himself that first babies often took a long time to deliver.

In the rush and excitement he hadn't noticed the man who'd followed him, after as foreman of the jury he'd delivered the verdict of guilty to the presiding judge. The same man who'd sat through the court procedures, who'd watched him standing at the vending machine, who'd followed him to the car park and who was now in a black car with tinted windows, following him as he raced towards the hospital.

Mother Nature opened her heavens and the rain began to pour, causing Darryl to slow a little as his windscreen steamed up and his vision was temporarily hindered.

The blunder was soon committed as he braked a little too heavily and over steered a little too much to the right on the bend of the rural valley road. The car slid to a halt in the ditch at the side of the road.

"Shit!" he shouted as he banged his fist with frustration on the steering wheel.

Movement caught his eye in the rear view mirror, as he saw a black car pull into the side of the road behind him. "Thank God," he said aloud. Hopefully whoever it was would assist him to get to the hospital.

A man approached the driver side of the car as Darryl started to climb out. "Thank God, I need to get to the hospital, my partner's about to give birth. Could you..." he stopped as he noticed the gun in the man's hand.

"You don't fuck with the mob," the man said as he raised the gun.

The horrific bang of the shot was the last thing Darryl was to ever hear in his life. Simultaneously his baby boy cried his first cry as he entered the world.

Assignment Fifty One - Carlos discovered (blank) under a pile of shoes in the back of his grandmothers closet

19th February 2021

J.M. wanted to explore her horror writing, and after some research, tapped into primal fears, which led to Michael being unable to sleep that night!

Michael had fun writing a piece of fan fiction, exploring the events around another famous wardrobe.

S.J. went all serious with a story regarding the horrifying discovery of a family secret.

Carlos and the Spider

By

J.M. McKenzie

Carlos knew Miranda would disapprove if he wore blue sneakers with a green shirt. But the only way to get them was to put his hand in the place where the spiders lurked.

Carlos discovered the spider under a pile of shoes in the back of his closet. He was blindly groping for the companion to his green sneaker, when he felt it crawl onto his hand and scurry up his arm. He dropped the sneaker and jumped back, shrieking, and shaking his arm furiously until it fell off.

"Arghh!"

He froze, glancing desperately around the room. Where was it? Where had it gone? The voile curtains billowed carelessly in the late summer breeze from the open window. The smell of Miranda's perfume lingered in the air, from where she had created a little mist cloud that she walked through before leaving the room. The room was immaculate as usual. A place for everything and everything in its place. Not many places for a spider to hide. Except possibly behind the scatter cushions, strategically placed on the matching bedspread? No, he was sure it fallen onto the floor.

His toes curled inside his socks, his feet suddenly horribly exposed and vulnerable. He resisted the urge to jump onto the bed like a cartoon damsel avoiding a mouse. Something tickled the back of his neck. He jumped and wriggled and shrieked again, slapping at his neck and shoulders with both hands.

Then he saw it.

It was on the floor between him and the door. Its black body stood out against the cream of the bedroom carpet. It wasn't moving but he knew that it would and when it did it would be fast.

He'd known there was gonna be one in there. He *knew* it. Right from when Miranda had looked him up and down and her nose had wrinkled when her eyes came to rest on his blue sneakers. He had known then exactly what was going to happen. She was gonna send him back up for the green sneakers and there would be a spider. It was as inevitable as the fact that she would make a show of flirting with him all night at the party, then complain of a headache as soon as they got home.

Ten minutes earlier, when he'd stood in front of the mirror in his khaki pants and green Ted Baker polo shirt, he'd had every intention of wearing the green sneakers. His blue ones were beside him on the bedroom floor, but her voice rang in his head, as clear as if she was standing behind him. *Blue and green should never be seen, Carlos.* But of course, she wasn't standing behind him. She was already waiting for him downstairs by the front door. Car keys in one hand, drumming the long red talons of the other on the hall table, like the snare drum in a marching band.

He'd found the left green sneaker at the front of the closet, but the right one was hiding somewhere amid the dark clutter at the back. Back where the spiders lived. He'd *almost* tried to find it. Without thinking, he'd reached into the closet then stopped and drew his hand back, as his snoozing terror of a lurking arachnid awoke with a start, screaming to be fed.

Carlos looked at the green sneaker. He looked at the dark space in the back of the closet. He looked at the blue sneakers, resting tantalizingly on the floor, lit up as if in a spotlight, by a shaft of early evening sunlight. He put them on and headed downstairs. She'd never notice. She was itching to get away. She hated being late.

But of course, she'd noticed and now, exactly as predicted, here he was in a barefoot stand-off with a spider. And it wasn't just any old spider. Oh, no! This was a spider the likes of which he hadn't encountered for some time. In fact, possibly like never before. This was one mean mother-fucking behemoth of a spider. It was dark and hairy with a fat, swollen belly. The span of its finger-like legs was almost as wide as his hand. Eight jet-black eyes as big as papaya seeds, watched him from the top of its furry head. Add in a couple of vicious yellow fangs, and its countenance was that of Beelzebub embodied.

"Carlos! Where are you? We need to *leave*. Now!" Miranda yelled up the stairs.

"Ok, Honey. Just looking for my green sneakers," Carlos yelled back, still staring at the spider.

He daren't let it out of his sight.

"Oh God! Just wear the brown ones. They're down here!"

Jesus! **Now** *she says just wear the brown ones!* "Ok, Honey. Thanks. I'll be down in a sec."

The bedroom door was wide open just a few feet in front of him. All he had to do was step over the spider, close the door, and go downstairs. How hard could it be?

He didn't move.

The spider watched him.

But then, it would still be in the room when they got back. By then, it could be anywhere. Under the bed. Back in the closet. Under the bedside cabinet. IN THE BED! When they got into bed and turned out the lights ... It didn't bear thinking about. Carlos shuddered at the thought of the spider crawling over his face while he slept.

"Carlos! Come ON!"

He stepped forward. The spider scuttled back a few inches, still keeping him in its sights.

He stepped to the side. The spider mirrored his movement.

Carlos's eyes flicked down to the green sneaker. It lay on its side just behind him to his left.

He could have sworn that the spider glanced towards it too.

He took a step back. The spider scurried forward. When he stopped, it stopped.

"CARLOS! NOW!"

He lunged for the sneaker. The spider rushed him.

He grabbed the sneaker and, in one movement, slapped it down hard on the fat hairy body moving rapidly towards him.

For a moment, time stood still.

Carlos stared in disgust at the ends of the splayed furry legs poking out from beneath the edges of the sneaker.

The air in the room felt thick. Oppressive. As if something was going to happen. Even the curtains stopped moving.

Then he saw movement. First from one side, and then from the other, a tiny, paler version of the spider emerged from under the sneaker and skittered towards him. One, two, three, four of them. He stumbled backwards. Five, six, seven! More and more of them streamed from under the sneaker. They were running across the carpet in all directions. Some ran onto his feet. Up his legs. They were on his chest, his arms, his neck, his face. *Oh, dear GOD!*

Carlos screamed. He screamed as he frantically brushed them off his body with his hands. They were everywhere. He screamed as he picked up the green sneaker and screamed again as he saw her ruined belly giving up the last trickle of her offspring. He continued to scream as he rushed around the room smashing at the spiders with the sneaker. He didn't stop until they were all gone.

By the time he was finished he was sweating and panting. He doubled over with his hands on his knees, to try and catch his breath, the splattered sneaker still clutched in his hand.

"Carlos, what *are* you doing?"

Miranda was standing in the doorway. Her face was a picture of astonishment, mixed with irritation.

"Sorry, Dear ... there was a ... spider," he said between gasps.

"Oh, Carlos." Miranda turned on her heel and disappeared.

Still holding the sneaker, Carlos followed her.

Five minutes later, they were in the car on the way to the party. Carlos was wearing the brown sneakers. Miranda was bristling beside him, her back straight and her features set. She stared straight ahead.

"I'm sorry, Dear," Carlos tried.

"Just drive, Carlos. We're already late."

Carlos focused on the road ahead.

A stray bead of sweat trickled down his forehead. He took one had off the steering wheel to wipe it away. But instead of melting away on his touch, it moved onto his finger. He looked at his hand. A small brown spider was perched on his knuckle, staring at him with eight tiny jet-black eyes.

Carlos screamed and shook his hand.

The spider ran up his arm and inside the sleeve of his shirt.

He screamed again and writhed in horror.

He could feel it moving around inside his shirt, across his chest, down his belly.

He tore at his shirt. The buttons popped.

Miranda was screaming now too, as the car careered from side to side across the road.

The last thing Carlos saw was the row of bright red chevrons on the warning sign ahead. Miranda's final scream pierced the night air as the car crashed through the barriers of the hairpin bend.

Grandma's Closet

By

Michael Andrews

Twelve-year-old Carlos is a lonely boy, but one with an active mind. He can create the wildest adventures with imaginary friends and deadly villains. A boring trip to his Grandma's gives him the perfect opportunity to "go on yet another adventure."

Carlos discovered what looked like a trapdoor under a pile of shoes in the back of his grandmother's closet. "What's this?" The twelve-year-old scratched his closely shaven head and looked around guiltily. He knew that he shouldn't be in his grandmother's room, but after listening to his mother and grandmother talk incessantly for nearly two hours, Carlos had decided to go exploring.

***

Grandmother's house was a huge mansion, sprawling across a six-acre estate. He'd already had many adventures within the woodlands in the grounds, but the drumming of raindrops against the windows had dissuaded him from venturing outside.

With only the inside of the mansion to explore, the skinny boy's laughter had filled the large hallway as he slid down the winding marble bannisters before Mr Garrity, the butler, had firmly told him that the stairway was not a playground.

Rubbing his backside from the slap he had received; he cursed his mother under his breath as he recalled her giving the old guy permission to punish him after he had been caught peeing into Grandma's Ming vase at the age of seven.

After searching through various rooms, Carlos had opened the door and found himself in his Grandma's bedroom. He gaped at the large, drape-covered four poster bed. The red velvet drapes were tied back against the pillars, showing a bedspread of golden and silver embroidery etched into a navy black blanket. His eyes were drawn to the intricate patterns and without realising, he had covered the short distance from the door and stood next to her bed. There was a soft toy nestled between the pillows. It was a small lion, one with a friendly face. He smiled as he recalled that it had accompanied him to bed from an early age whenever he stayed over.

Carlos knew that he was in dangerous territory. The one thing told to him from an early age was to "never, and I mean ever!" go into Grandma's bedroom. He felt a tingle in his mind and looked down. His right hand was running across the patterns of the bedspread and a window in his mind seemed to open. He seemed to see a young girl; she was pretty, platinum white hair and pale skin and she was looking back at him.

Come to me, Carlos. Find me and help me.

"What?" he spluttered out, turning around to see who had crept up on him. The doorway was empty.

Carlos, I need your help. Please come and rescue me.

"Who are you? Where are you?" Carlos felt his blood beginning to pump through his body as he realised that he was going to go on another adventure. He smiled to himself and pulled his shirt from his shorts, ready for whatever action lay before him.

"Where are you?" he frowned, looking around. "I can't help you if I don't know where you are!"

Carlos heard a faint click and spun to his left. An old wooden closet door had come ajar and he smiled to himself. He opened the door wider and was disappointed to see a wardrobe full of clothes and shoes. A faint smell of camphor masked what the boy assumed to be sweaty shoes.

"Urgh! Grandma's feet smell!" Carlos giggled as he held his hand over his mouth, pretending to gag at the imagined smell of his Grandma's toes. He brushed aside the heavy coats and saw the back of the cupboard. Stepping inside, he knocked loudly on the wood.

"Ow!" Carlos licked his bruised knuckles as they bounced off the heavy oak and he turned to climb back out. His foot caught on a shoe and he slipped, falling to the floor of the large, walk-in closet. He moaned and rubbed his head where he had stumbled, his head bouncing off one of the wooden shelves that held even more of Grandma's shoes. His eyes glazed for a moment.

Help me Carlos. Save me. Rescue me.

Carlos shook his head, his vision clearing.

"What's this?" the twelve-year-old said as he scratched his closely shaven head and looked around guiltily. Smiling that no-one had heard his fall, he examined the newly uncovered floor of the closet and saw what looked like a trap door. His excitement began to build again as he knew, he just knew that he was going to go on another adventure.

Clearing the shoes away from the trapdoor, Carlos saw a silver ring embedded into the dark oak panelling.

Congratulating himself that he had not bitten his nails for two whole weeks, he managed to pick at the metal ring until he levered it upwards and he pushed two fingers through the loop. Pulling it, the wooden trapdoor stubbornly refused to move.

"Okay, let's do this properly," the boy grinned to himself. Standing behind the door, he pushed fingers from both hands through the silver ring and heaved. Sweat began to drip from his brow and his small biceps strained before he let go, slumping backwards.

"Bloody hell, that's heavy!" he panted. His right hand rested against a piece of cotton and he picked it up, wiping his face. He glanced downwards.

"Oh gross!" he yelled, throwing the pair of black cotton underwear out of the cupboard. A silly little chuckle escaped his mouth. "I've just wiped my face with Grandma's undies! YUK!" The boy spat onto the palm of his hand and wiped it over his face, getting rid of any "Granny Germs" that may have lingered on the underwear. "At least they were clean... I hope!"

Carlos. I need you. Help me.

"Oh right!" he frowned. He positioned himself over the metal ring, bending his knees and slipped as many fingers through the hole as he could. Bracing himself, he lifted and was surprised that this time, the trapdoor lifted, slowly at first, but then he managed to pull it all the way open and leaned it against the back of the closet with a solid thunk.

Darkness stared up at Carlos. He scratched his head, peering down into pitch black.

"That's impossible," he muttered. He knew that something was wrong, very wrong, but his childish sense of adventure got the better of him. He placed a foot inside and found a step. Steadying himself, he lifted his left foot and found a second step, some six inches below the first. His right foot found the third.

Tensing himself, he looked back over his shoulder at the light from Grandma's bedroom. "Let's do this!" Left foot, right foot, left foot, right foot. Further and further down the staircase the boy went until his head was below the bottom of the closet.

BANG!

The trapdoor swung shut, leaving Carlos in total darkness. Momentary panic set in before he calmed his breathing. He stretched out his hands to each side. His left hand touched a stone wall and he felt along it, slowly stepping downwards into the unknown.

"ARGH!" Carlos cried out as he felt spiderwebs brush across his face. "Please don't be Shelob! Please don't be Shelob!"

Visions of the huge spider from the Lord of the Rings flashed through his mind. In his fear, he placed his left foot a fraction further forward than it should have been, and it slipped over the edge of the step. He put his arms out in front of himself to protect his body against the fall, but his feet found a dusty floor just another step down.

"Stupid, stupid!" Carlos cursed himself. "Frodo wouldn't act like that!"

Glancing around in the darkness, he spotted a faint, red light to the right and he edged himself to the wall. Using it as guidance, he crept slowly towards the light, pleased that it seemed to be getting brighter and larger with each onward step.

Finally, he saw the mouth of the cave, and he rushed forwards, pleased to be away from the monster spiders that he was sure that he had felt crawling over him. He looked himself over and was surprised to see that his shorts and shirt had somehow changed into a rustic tunic, cotton leggings that covered his thin but muscular legs, and leather sandals in place of his trainers.

"Here now! Who are you and where have you been, boy?" A commanding voice jolted him back to awareness and he stared up at the mounted knight on a pristine white stallion. But it wasn't a stallion.

"That's... a... Pegasus!" Carlos spluttered out, his voice dripping with awe. He raised a shaky hand towards the magnificent animal.

"Of course it is." The knight looked at him as if he was the village idiot. "All royal steeds are from the mighty line of Barroc. Now, answer my questions or feel the back of my hand."

"I'm, er..." Carlos stuttered.

The knight started to dismount, but then his eyes clouded over. Shaking his head, he looked down at the young boy, his stern expression having softened. "Squire Carlos, why didn't you tell me that Her Highness had sent you to gather some herbs?"

"Erm, because she said not to tell anyone," the boy lied, hoping that he could wander away from the knight.

"You appear empty handed." The knight dismounted and Carlos cringed, expecting the tall man to strike him. However, he found his small hand clasped into the metal gauntlet of the knight and was led towards the nearby copse of trees. "Princess Jadis needs the herbs urgently. Come, let us gather them and return to the castle."

A confused but relieved Carlos quickly picked an armful of plants, hoping that they looked like herbs. The knight seemed not to be paying attention to what it was that the boy was gathering, just that he was actually picking a bunch.

Do not concern yourself with Sir Harley. He is under my command and will guide you to me.

Breathing a little easier, reassured by the strange girl's voice, Carlos followed the knight back to his steed and allowed the strong man to lift him into the saddle, before mounting the pegasus himself.

"Hold tight," Sir Harley chuckled. "If you've never flown before, it can be scary."

Carlos wanted to reply but found that his breath was taken away by a combination of the strong grip around his waist by Sir Harley, but more so by the quickly disappearing ground as the Pegasus soared into the air.

Wind buffeted Carlos's face and he couldn't help but grin as he looked down and saw the green landscape flying past below. He could see herds of horses running across the plains, and small villages dotted around the crop filled fields.

"This is amazing!" the boy crowed, giggling with joy as he saw sights that he never believed that he would see in his young life.

A deep rumble filled the air. The temperature dropped suddenly, and the wind picked up. The Pegasus threw its' head back and Sir Harley fought with the reins, keeping the steed on course. Carlos felt himself slip slightly in the saddle, but the strong grip of the knight held him in place.

"What's happening?" Carlos shouted, trying to be heard over the howling wind.

"It's the Empress," Sir Harley shouted. "She knows that you are coming to save Princess Jadis and is trying to stop us."

"What?" Carlos felt his body shiver against the onslaught of the now driving rain which was quickly turning into sleet.

"Princess Jadis is a prisoner in her own palace at the hands of her older sister," Sir Harley hissed. "She's a wicked, tyrannical woman who wants to kill her younger, prettier sister."

"Then we've got to help Jadis!" Carlos crowed. He looked for a sword to hold aloft, like the movie heroes always did, but only had the flowers. He groaned as the strong wind blew off the heads of the flowers, and he slumped backwards, resting against the cold, metal steel of Sir Harley's armour.

"No matter, young squire," the knight reassured him, patting the young boy's cotton clad leg. "You are the flower that Jadis has been waiting for."

Sleep my Carlos, my flower. Sleep.

And sleep Carlos did.

As the light shone through the window arch, Carlos awoke, struggling with the heavy bedsheets. He pushed them to one side, exposing his pale body. He looked around the room and saw nothing that he recognised. A white vase. A crystal decanter of an orange liquid with two glass goblets set to one side. The boy stretched, pushing the bedclothes from his body.

I didn't realise you were so cute... so young.

Carlos looked down, grabbing the bedclothes to cover himself. He was dressed only in a pair of cotton pants that stretched halfway to his knees. Looking around for the girl, he saw that he was alone in the room.

"Where are you?" he asked aloud, feeling a little self-conscious that he was talking to himself.

Come to me in the highest tower. Rescue me, Carlos.

Carlos quickly dressed in the clean clothes that he found hanging over the back of a chair beside the bed. He tied the leather strapping to fix the leggings around his thin waist before noticing a rapier-like sword leaning against the wall. He picked it up and swung it back and forth, before performing a smooth dance just as Syrio Forel had done on the episode of Game of Thrones that he had sneakily watched without his parents' knowledge.

Finally, he strapped the belt around his waist and put the sword through the loop. He stumbled the first few steps towards the door before he got used to the weight and balance of having the weapon at his side and he opened the door cautiously. Not knowing if he was a guest or a captive, he peered his head out into the corridor.

Pleased to see that the door was unguarded, he walked to the left and up a winding stone staircase. Round and around he climbed, and he felt his legs start to tire. He paused at a window and looked out. He could see different spires of the castle that he was in, and beyond the walls, a city stretched out as far as he could see.

The call of seagulls drew his attention to a coastline. White sand lay next to a sapphire sea. Boats of various size sailed back and forth, some with as many as five masts, white billowing sails moving them along the coast.

"I'm not in Kansas anymore," Carlos chuckled.

"No, you're not. You are in the Empire of Charn."

Carlos turned quickly, so fast that he stumbled and nearly lost his balance. A tall, dark haired woman stared coldly at him. His eyes were drawn to the golden tiara that glistened in the sunlight from the window, but there was no sparkle in her eyes. Black pools of hatred stared back at him.

"Erm... where?"

"You have been brought here by evil means," the woman said, reaching out for his arm. "I will send you back from whence you came."

Carlos. Help me! She is the evil Empress who has imprisoned me.

He jumped back, out of her reach. "I'm here to rescue the princess," he shouted before turning and running up the remaining stairs. Heavy footsteps followed him and he heard the swearing of guards as they struggled to keep up with the fleet-footed youth.

A large, wooden door blocked his escape from the oncoming soldiers and he grabbed the handle. Frantically turning it, he found that it was locked.

Carlos. Save me. Rescue me.

"I'm trying, Jadis. But the door is locked."

There is a key hanging to the side.

Sure enough, as Carlos's gaze was drawn to the left, a large metal key hung on a nail that had been driven into the stone wall. He reached for it but dropped it through shaking fingers. Scrambling around on the floor, he picked it up just as the first guard rounded the final bend of the staircase.

"Stop boy!" he shouted. "You can't let her out."

"It's cruel and wrong!" Carlos shouted back. "I'll save you, princess!"

Putting the key into the lock, he turned it just as the guard wrestled him away. As the two sprawled on the floor, the Empress caught up with them, staring in horror at the slowly opening door.

"What have you done?" she cried. "You've killed us all."

"I've freed the young princess," Carlos crowed as he saw the girl from his vision step through the doorway.

"Jadis, stop..." the Empress said as the young girl smiled back at her.

"Thank you, Carlos. I knew I could count on the bravery of a son of Adam."

The air around the young girl shimmered and, in her place, stood a woman of perfect beauty. Long blonde hair flowed down a jet-black dress. She held out her hand and a beam of light shot from her fingers, burning the guard to a crisp.

Carlos yelped as he felt his own skin burn and jumped away from the now dead guard. Looking up at the fully grown woman, he asked "Er... Princess Jadis?"

"Hush now, Carlos," Jadis smiled down at him. "Come and stand by my side."

"Boy. Stay where you are," the Empress said. "She will use your soul strength for evil."

"You are the only evil one here," Carlos snapped and hurried over to stand by the side of the blonde-haired woman. He felt her take his hand and she started to talk in a language that he had never heard before. His body started to tingle, and his eyelids began to feel heavy.

"Jadis, no! That spell is forbidden." The Empress reached out to her sister.

"Nothing is forbidden to me." Jadis smiled as a green light enveloped her body.

Carlos felt as though he was being turned inside out and tried to pull away from the woman but her grip was too tight.

"Thank you, son of Adam. You have given me the power that I need to destroy this world!" She clapped her hand and spoke a Deplorable Word.

Carlos staggered away as a thunderbolt of energy erupted from the two. He watched in horror as the Empress and her guards turned to dust.

Jadis turned to him, leaning forwards to bring her face to his. "Thank you for freeing me, Carlos. Your work here is done. Tell your Grandmother I said hello."

He felt her lips on his forehead. They were soft and damp...

***

"Carlos? Carlos, are you okay?"

The boy groaned as he felt a wet cloth on his forehead. Opening his eyes, he sat up and instantly regretted it.

"Easy there boy," Mr Garrity said, picking the boy up easily from the bottom of the closet. "You've had a nasty bump there." He laid the boy gently on the bed, under the careful watch of Grandma Lucy.

"I'm back?" Carlos smiled as he felt himself sink into the soft covers.

"You've not been anywhere, lad," Mr Garrity smiled at him, stroking his head gently as he stepped away to let the boy's mother begin to fuss over him.

"I went to Charn, and met a knight, and flew on a Pegasus, and met a princess." Carlos realised how crazy he sounded. "I did, didn't I?"

"You slipped and banged your head," Carlos's mother frowned. "I thought it may knock some sense into you, but no, another wild story!"

"It seemed so real! But I must have been gone for hours. How didn't you notice?"

"It has been five minutes since Mr Garrity told you off for playing on the staircase," his mother said, concern now evident on her face. Maybe he had done some damage to his head.

"I guess so, but maybe she magicked time when she sent me back."

"Who sent you back, dear?" Grandma Lucy asked, as she handed the boy the cuddly lion.

"The princess did. Princess Jadis was locked in a tower, but I rescued her, and she killed the evil Empress to become Queen. She said to say hello to you, Grandma Lucy. Oh, hello Aslan." Carlos spilled the words so quickly as he cuddled the soft toy that it took a moment for the meaning to dawn on Grandma Lucy.

Lucy Pevensie narrowed her eyes and grasped the hand of her grandson. "Jadis? The White Witch?" She felt a chill run through her body.

Oh, my little Lucy. How the fates conspire to twist the destinies of our families together. We will meet in my future and your past. Only this time, with the foreknowledge I have from your grandson, Aslan will not be able to save you.

"I need to call Peter, Edmund and Susan!"

The Box in the Closet
By
S.J. Gibbs

Carlos finds a box in his grandmother's closet. Can the contents of one box change his life forever?

Carlos discovered a box under a pile of shoes in the back of his grandmother's closet.

If only he had been more understanding of the troubled woman, she might still be alive.

All of her beautiful flowers were in bloom now in the garden. How she'd loved to be outside pottering around. It was her pride and joy. Her piece of heaven she'd called it.

He knew she'd harboured secrets from her past, but to her dying breath she'd remained silent, unable to release whatever it was, which had troubled her soul.

She'd been a solitary figure, with no friends, but he'd loved spending his summer holidays from school at her beautiful cottage on the Cornwall coast. His parents worked long hours, so they were grateful to his grandmother for taking care of him.

He pulled the box further into the room, from underneath the pile of shoes.

Intrigued as to what maybe concealed in the sealed box, he rapidly hunted around for a pair of scissors to break the seal. Carefully he cut away at the masking tape, until he was able to peer inside. Documents and plenty of them greeted his eyes.

His grandfather had died before he'd even been born. This he knew, but nobody ever talked about it or discussed it. It was a taboo subject, one he'd learned never to ask questions about.

Would an explanation around his grandfather's death lie amongst these papers?

His grandmother had died five months ago and had left Carlos, the cottage and all of her belongings. As an artist, he'd decided to uproot his life from London and move into the cottage he so loved.

He'd been at the cottage for a few weeks now and had slowly cleared out the belongings he didn't want to keep. The closet in his grandmother's bedroom being one of the last places, which needed clearing. Her clothes and shoes had seemed so personal, which was the reason he'd left it until now. A painful awareness of how much she'd suffered towards the end over came him as soon as he'd entered her bedroom.

He removed the top document from the box and began to read.

Written across the top was the word 'Geburtsregister.' His eyes scanned the rest of the document, which appeared to be somebody's birth certificate. The entries were as follows: -

Heiner Vinzenz Wolff (mannlich)

16/10/1921 Munich

Vater – Falk Meinhard Wolff – Arzt – Zweibruckenstrasse 32

Mutter – Hilda Prinz -21- Verheiratet

It was beyond Carlos's abilty to understand. Why would his grandmother have a German birth certificate belonging to somebody named Heiner Wolff.

His mind started to work overtime. He knew his grandfather had died in 1980 at the age of 59. Quickly, he did the sums in his head. 1921, his grandfather would have been born in 1921, the same year as this Heiner Wolff, but who was this Heiner Wolff?

A thousand thoughts shuffled through his brain like a pack of playing cards.

The quietness and seclusion of the cottage struck him at once. Why had his grandmother chosen to live in such isolation? Why would she want to do that?

He couldn't change what he had seen, but he was terrified to look any further into the box for fear of what he may discover. Closing the lid to the box, he pushed it away from him with his foot and headed to the kitchen to make a coffee.

After 50 minutes of contemplation, he phoned his mother.

His heart quickened as he asked the question, "Why would grandma have a German birth certificate for somebody named Heiner Wolff, the same age as my grandfather?"

She sounded angry, "I've told you before not to ask questions about him."

"But I need answers, we can't just keep pretending like he never existed," he ran his fingers through his hair.

"Take my advice, whatever you've found, just leave well alone," she ended the call.

Why was she always so reluctant to talk about his grandfather? Not at all sure he was making a wise decision, Carlos went back upstairs, for further inspection of the contents of the box.

The next document was another birth certificate for a female, Friede Loris, German birthplace again, but this time the birth year was the same as his grandma's. It made no sense.

His mind objected at first, but finally submitted to the fact that these could possibly be the birth certificates of his grandparents. He took a deep breath.

He made himself comfortable in the upholstered armchair by the window and delved further into the box, sending up a little prayer as he did so.

The next few papers were a bewildering assortment of coded letters and symbols. He had no idea what they were. Just exactly what were the secrets his grandma had kept so close to her chest?

He hesitated, before delving any deeper into the box.

What was the link here?

He couldn't sit on the fence any longer; it was time to find the answers.

His optimistic attitude began to falter as he pulled out a sealed envelope with his name written on the front in his grandmother's distinct writing style.

Carlos liked being in control, but he had none in this situation as he carefully opened the envelope, afraid of the secrets, which may or may not be about to release themselves from whatever was held within.

The impact of the words she may have left behind for him was something he now braced himself for as he began to read the letter his grandma knew would be discovered after her death.

He began to read: -

My dear Carlos,

Until I was 16 years old my family lived in Munich. They were cheerful times; I was a child carefree, unaware of what my future was to hold.

I am so sorry that I never found the courage to tell you of my life and your Grandfather's before my passing. I was too fearful of your rejection.

I was sixteen when I met your Grandfather; he towered above me, the muscles in his arms and shoulders strained against his shirt. When he asked me to dance for the first time, I was in love with him instantly. We were married by the time I was 18 he was 20.

It was a happy time but not for long as Germany was already at war. Our real names are Heiner Vinzenz Wolff and my maiden name was Friede Loris before I became Friede Wolff.

It wasn't long before our lives were under assault and your Grandfather was recruited into the German army.

I was unaware at the time that he was soon made an officer of the S.S. and was posted to Auschwitz, a concentration camp in Poland. I remained in Germany, throughout the war.

It was only after the war was over that I learned of the terrible things, which had happened to the prisoners in the camps. I was disgusted to think that my husband, your Grandfather had been involved in such atrocities.

He had changed too; he was never the same as the lovely young man I'd married. He had terrible mood swings, drunk heavily and carried an awful amount of guilt and terror within his memories.

We changed our names, invented false identities and moved to England, in the hope of starting afresh. The memories never left your Grandfather and eventually he took his own life.

At this stage I told your Mother and we agreed to never discuss the subject again.

I apologize once more my darling Carlos, for you to have to learn that you are most unfortunately a Nazi descendant.

Please forgive me in your heart,

Your loving and doting Grandma.

Carlos dropped the letter to the floor, his hand trembling. His own world had just crashed around him.

His mind rushed to the knowledge of Auschwitz and the gas chambers. It had been a place like Hell. Guilt rushed over him, even though he knew there was no reason he should bear any guilt. Shame for what his family, his grandfather, did to thousands of other families. How could he ever come to terms with this? Why was he alive, when so many had died? This would hang over him for the rest of his life. One thing he knew for sure he would never ever have contact with his own mother again. His life was destroyed.

Bile accumulated n his throat and he rushed to the bathroom to vomit.

How was it possible that his grandfather had been so sadistic? Tens of thousands of Jews had been killed, and he had been part of that war machine. The full horror of the crimes raced through his mind. Physically it was as though he'd been struck with a huge stick over and over.

How could he correct this? What drastic action could he take?

He dialled his GP, "I would like to book an appointment to get sterilised," he heard himself say.

One thing he knew for sure was that he would end this bloodline right here.

Assignment Fifty Two - Lena was raised on violin lessons and minimal parental supervision

19th March 2021

J.M. continued her horror practice, pushing the boundaries of writing with the creation of an evil child.

Michael wrote an experimental piece, exploring a catfish scenario, in a story about online grooming. As such, some readers will find the piece upsetting.

S.J. showed how subjective writing can be, with a story in the style of historical fiction. It showed her varied reading choices. However, she does feel that the ending is quite weak, something that she acknowledges is a development area.

Lena

By

J.M. McKenzie

There's something not right about Lena, but Elizabeth just can't put her finger on what it is ...

Lena was raised on violin lessons and minimal parental supervision. She was, to all intents and purposes, a beautiful child. Her almond shaped, cobalt blue eyes sparkled like ice against the pale perfection of her small, sharp features. The lines and angles of her poker straight, white-blond bob, framed her face in a way that was both pleasing in its geometric neatness, and alarming in its unnatural regularity.

The hair could be a metaphor for the child herself, Elizabeth thought, as she watched her play a set of faultless arpeggios in front of the open bay window, beside the baby grand piano. The music room was small and circular, and the large window occupied half the wall space. It was a warm spring day and the full-length, white lace curtains wafted in the breeze, revealing glimpses of pristine white garden furniture on the striped front lawn. Somewhere in the distance a mower buzzed, and the smell of freshly cut grass drifted in. A skylark trilled, as if offering a harmony to the delicate notes that Lena played with a skill that far exceeded that expected of her nine and a half years.

The child was so immaculate in every way that it was disconcerting. She played effortlessly. She looked exquisite. She spoke and behaved impeccably. But there something missing. Beneath all the beauty and perfection something was off. Not enough to be obvious, or even to identify, but just enough to notice if, like the garden furniture, you were looking in the right direction at right moment.

Lena, completed the exercise and lowered the violin, looking expectantly at Elizabeth.

"Well done, Lena," she said, and smiled at the girl.

The girl smiled back. Her face transformed into a mask of happiness. But that was all it was. A mask. Her features moved in all the right ways. Her soft, pink lips parted as they curved upwards, revealing her small, sparkling white teeth. Her button nose wrinkled, and the corners of her eyes creased. But, despite all that, there was absolutely no warmth in the smile. No warmth at all. Lena's perfect smile was as cold as her ice blue eyes.

Elizabeth shuddered. That was it. Now that she thought about it, in the few short weeks she had known her, Lena had exhibited such a complete lack of warmth or emotion, in any circumstance whatsoever, that it was startling. It was more than startling. It was frightening.

"Are you alright, Miss Aldershaw?" Lena asked, with a look of concern.

No. Not concern, more ... curiosity.

Elizabeth gathered herself. Avoiding eye contact with the child, she smiled again and straightened her back.

"Of course, Lena. Why do you ask?"

"You just seemed a bit distracted for a moment. As if someone had ... walked over your grave."

Elizabeth flinched, as if she had been physically struck. Was it her imagination, or did these dark blue eyes glint with malevolence when she said the words *your grave*?

"No," she said, her voice higher than she meant it to be as she tried to give the impression of lightness. "Of course not, Lena. I was just … enjoying your beautiful playing."

Lena smiled that smile again. "Why thank you, Miss Aldershaw."

"As I said before, Lena, you don't have to call me Miss Aldershaw. Elizabeth is fine."

"Oh, Miss Aldershaw, but I *prefer* to call you by your correct name. If you don't mind that is? It just seems more … *correct*. It shows how much I respect you, and I *do* respect you, Miss Aldershaw. I *really* do."

"That's fine, Lena. Don't worry about it."

"Oh, I'm not *worrying* about it, Miss Aldershaw. I can assure you …"

Elizabeth cut her off. "I know, Lena. It was just a figure of speech. Shall we carry on?"

"Oh yes, Miss Aldershaw. Yes please."

"So, could you have a go at the Handel piece we started in our last lesson? The Sonata II in G minor?"

"Of course, Miss Aldershaw." Lena started rifling through the papers on the piano.

Elizabeth watched as she positioned the pages of the sheet music on the stand and prepared to play.

She felt oddly unnerved. Her mouth was dry, and her heart pounded in her chest. What was wrong with her? She was just a child!

Lena began to play. Like everything else about her, she played with technical brilliance but with absolutely no emotion whatsoever.

Elizabeth's thoughts began to drift.

She knew she was the latest in a long line of violin teachers. She had asked about Lena's previous tutelage to get an idea of where she was, and what had been covered so far. The response from Lena's mother had been vague, to say the least.

"Oh, you know how it is." she had chirped. "These peripatetic music teachers come and go. We've had a few over the years. Some good. Some less so. Some Lena didn't *get along* with. Some who didn't *get along* with her."

She smiled at Lena, but her face was tight. Her features looked uncomfortable.

Lena smiled back at her mother.

Her mother looked away quickly.

At the time, Elizabeth had thought that the look that passed between mother and daughter had been conspiratorial. Now, she saw it for what it was. Fear. Lena's mother was afraid of her nine-year-old daughter.

Suddenly, Elizabeth wanted the lesson to be over. She wanted to get out of this beautiful house and garden, and away from this perfect child with her cold blue eyes and her chilling smile. As far away as she could get.

"Are you *sure* you're alright, Miss Aldershaw?" Lena had stopped playing again. Her eyes were fixed on Elizabeth's. "You don't *seem* alright to me."

"Of course, I am, Lena. Please carry on." Elizabeth's voice trembled. Her heart was beating so fast and loud now that she feared Lena would hear it. She didn't know why, but she just knew that wouldn't be good. Some ancient instinct was telling her not to let Lena sense her fear.

"You don't *sound* alright, Miss Aldershaw," Lena said, and put the violin gently down on the piano.

"I'm *perfectly* fine, Lena!"

"I do hope you're not going to be like the … *others*, Miss Aldershaw." She took a step towards Elizabeth. Smiling. The bow rested loosely in her hand.

"Lena, please continue with the piece." Elizabeth swallowed hard. The words seemed to stick in her throat. She took a step back.

"We just didn't *get along*, you see," Lena said. She ran her finger along the length of the bow.

"Oh," she said and looked down at her finger. A drop of bright red blood formed on its tip and dropped to the floor.

To Elizabeth it seemed to happen in slow motion. The bloom of blood. The drip. The small splatter as it hit the floor. She looked at the bow. The hairs were synthetic, she knew that. But to cut her finger? It wasn't possible! They must be razor sharp. Who would give a child a bow like …

Lena flicked the bow across Elizabeth's throat. There was no pain, just a brief cold sensation, followed by a gush of warmth that flowed down her chest. She put her hand to her neck and then looked at the sticky red liquid on her fingers in confusion. Her knees buckled and she sank to the floor. Her vision dimmed and her head was filled with sound of her own blood whooshing in her ears. The whoosh gave way to a fast and thready flutter. The flutter slowed to a soft pulse. The pulse slowed. Stuttered. Stopped.

The last thing Elizabeth heard was the sound of Lena's mothers voice as she entered the room.

"Lena! Not again! What have you *done*?"

"I'm sorry, Mother. It's just that we weren't *getting along* ..."

Lena's Lessons in Life

By

Michael Andrews

Lena hated her violin lessons but was forced to endure them, along with many other miseries. Could she find her own enjoyment without any parent finding out?

Lena was raised on violin lessons and minimal parental supervision. From the age of eight, she was forced upstairs straight after school to practice. She dreaded the end of her practice as she heard the door to her bedroom open when Freddy, her thirteen-year-old brother, would come in to listen to the end of whichever piece she was playing. She tried to block the memories of what happened once she finished, but she still had the overriding feelings of guilt and dirtiness.

When Lena turned thirteen, Freddy had been murdered. The police said that he had been stabbed by another boy who was never caught. His death was a relief to Lena, but she had felt a burden of secrecy fall upon her and she knew that she could never tell her absent parents the truth.

Coming home after another long day at school, she rushed upstairs and completed the hour-long practice, hitting each note perfectly. Her parents would be so proud; if they cared that was. Putting down the hated instrument, Lena giggled as her bed bounced underneath her as she flopped down, kicking off the shiny black shoes that she wore to school.

This happened every day. Once she had scurried through the front door home from school, she hurried upstairs to her room to get through the horrid hour of violin practice before she started her troll through that day's homework, and then tried relaxing to do her own thing.

As she lay on her bed, her blonde hair spread across the pillows, she picked up her phone and logged into the chat app that she had installed the previous night. She snickered to herself as it loaded up, wondering who would be online. She knew that it was naughty but that was the new intoxicating addiction to her. She had heard about the rumours from the girls at school about this app and who were finding out about sex, having sexual conversations with boys from their school, and even exchanging naughty pictures.

Her memory flicked back to the sleepovers with her best friend Nettie, quietly discussing boys and how hot they were, exploring each other's young bodies, while fantasising about Lucas Harris, the cutest boy in their year. Lena had been in lust with Lucas since they had been ten, but Nettie was the one who had snared him.

Lena had resented Nettie for a few days, knowing that her friend was the object of her crush's desire, but had grudgingly forgiven her. She had tried a few times to snatch him away from Nettie, but he had shunned her publicly and she never forgave him. He must have upset Nettie as well as he stopped coming to school soon after. Lena remembered that his parents moved away, something about concentrating on their family, or at least their other son.

Sighing at the memory, she logged into the app. It asked questions such as her name, age, interests and for a profile picture. She scooted from her bed to her dressing table and looked into the mirror. She brushed her hair and picked up her lipstick. Satisfied with the result, she took several selfies before scrolling through all the pictures that she had taken of herself previously and selected the perfect one and uploaded it to the app. She smiled to herself and thought about how young she looked. It would drive the boys wild; she just knew it.

Snuggling down next to Jerry, her favourite bear, she started to flick through the profiles that were presented to her. Boys from the age of ten popped up and she frowned, her button nose screwing up in disgust. Finding the filter options, she quickly added a minimum age of fourteen, before changing it back down to thirteen. Lena remembered that some of her friends' younger brothers were little cuties. It would be such fun to tease the younger boys.

<PING>

<PING>

<PING>

<PING>

A stream of message notifications popped up and Lena scrolled through them before selecting one.

ANTBOI: Hi there. You're real pretty.

Lena clicked on his profile. A boy's face stared back at her. He had piercing blue eyes, brown hair parted down the middle and a spread of freckles across his nose and cheeks.

L-GIRL: Thnx. You're cute too. How old r u?

ANTBOI: I'm 13. U?

L-GIRL: I'm 15. Hope you don't mind me being older?

ANTBOI: Nah, that's kewl. It's my first time on here. Wot bout u?

L-GIRL: Me2 lol.

ANTBOI: I've never really chatted to a girl before. I'm a bit nervous.

L-GIRL: Aw that's so cute. I've never been with a boy, but I have chatted with boys before. Don't be scared.

ANTBOI: Thanks L. You're really kewl. Most of my mates call me gay cos I've never had a girlfriend but it's just that I'm scared.

L-GIRL: Why are you scared? You're a really cute boy. Have you got any more pics?

ANTBOI: Yeah... you really think I'm cute? [giggle]

L-GIRL: OGY!

ANTBOI: Wot?

L-GIRL: Oh god yeah! Can't believe you've got no gf! You a hottie!

<PING>

<PING>

<PING>

Lena felt her body tingle as she opened the pictures from the boy. Two pictures were of his face and she recognised him as Anthony White, a boy from Year 9. She had seen him around the school. He was on the fringes of the popular kids without being front and centre.

The third picture made her moan out loud as she saw his thin body clad only in a tight speedo.

L-GIRL: OMG! You're so cute. You're in the swim team, aren't you?

ANTBOI: Haha. Yeah. I hate the swimsuit. Much prefer shorts.

L-GIRL: No way. You're so cute.

Lena laid back on her bed and slipped a hand underneath her blouse. Teasing her body, she continued to chat to Anthony for another twenty minutes, slowly building up his confidence. Undoing her blouse, she snapped a couple of pictures of her own, underdeveloped breasts and sent them to him, before signing off.

Three days later, Lena was beginning to worry. She had seen Anthony around school, but he had not been back online and as she finished her violin practice, she nervously logged on to the app. She had started to look at other boys, but her heart pined for the cute Year 9 boy that she felt she'd had an immediate connection with.

<PING>

Warmth flooded through Lena as she opened the message.

ANTBOI: Really sorry. I got in a fight at school and the rents took my fone off me.

L-GIRL: Is it locked? They don't know about us chatting do they?

Lena felt a trickle of sweat run down her neck onto her breast. She slipped a hand inside her top and began to rub her nipple. It had already hardened with the thought of speaking with her new boyfriend, and she let out a little groan once more at the thought that Anthony's parents may know about them. Her fantasies had started to gain momentum over the last few days, and she felt her groin tingle in the anticipation of meeting the boy in person.

ANTBOI: I'm not stupid lol. Even if they break my pin, the app is hidden and encrypted.

L-GIRL: That's kewl. I have seen you around school. I wanted to come and say hi but my friends wouldn't think it's kewl.

ANTBOI: I thought you were at my school. I haven't seen you, but I guess your mates would diss you for being into a Year 9. I mean, you must be so kewl. I still can't believe that you're chatting to me but it would be so kewl if we cud meet sometime.

L-GIRL: I'd love that! But until we can, can you send me some more pics?

\<PING\>

\<PING\>

\<PING\>

\<PING\>

\<PING\>

Lena opened up the photos and, while they showed off his young smooth body, she felt disappointed that they didn't show more.

L-GIRL: How about some more that are a bit naughty lol?

ANTBOI: Urm... I dunno. Isn't that wrong?

L-GIRL: It's only me... I won't show them to anyone. I'll send you some as well, okay?

Lena waited, her breathing heavy with lust and anticipation. Had she pushed him too fast? She could see the three dots on the conversation bar, showing that Anthony was typing, or at least thinking about it.

ANTBOI: Okay. You first though.

Lena's finger slipped underneath her panties and found her groin. Teasing it around, she pulled up the pictures that she had prepared and sent four pictures, two of her small breasts and two of her shaven vagina.

Minutes passed. Again, bad thoughts ran through her mind. Should she be doing this? After all, he was younger than her, he was only thirteen. Her finger hovered over the close button, ready to cancel the app and delete the data.

<PING>

ANTBOI: Wow! That's so hot. I've never seen one before.

L-GIRL: [giggles] can I see yours?

ANTBOI: You won't share it anywhere will you? Or laugh?

L-GIRL: Never. I really like you Ant. I'd never hurt you.

<PING>

Lena's finger shook as it pushed the incoming notification. She gasped out loud as she saw a full body shot of the young boy. He was perfect. She knew in that moment that she was in love and had found her own Lucas, a better version of Lucas. She didn't need that slimeball that had shagged her at Nettie's fifteenth birthday party and then bragged about it to his friends. Anthony was a sensitive boy, a cute boy, a boy that she could mould to her desires and her wishes.

L-GIRL: Oh wow. Oh my god. You are beautiful.

ANTBOI: [blush] I'm not too small down there?

L-GIRL: It makes you even more perfect. We have gotta get together, if you want to that is?

ANTBOI: Really? I'd love that!

L-GIRL: How about tomorrow after school. Meet me at Highfields Park and we can like, kiss and stuff.

ANTBOI: Aw man, that's so hot thinking of it.

L-GIRL: Show me.

<PING>

L-GIRL: Tomorrow. 3.30. By the old oak tree. Wear your speedos under your school trousers.

ANTBOI: Erm...

L-GIRL: For me. Please. You're so cute.

ANTBOI: Okay [giggle]

Lena logged off, undressed, and got into bed. Flicking through the pictures of her new lover, well he was going to be, wasn't he? She drifted off to sleep.

Anthony tugged on his school tie, hating how it seemed to strangle him. He wiped his hands on his grey school trousers, leaving a small patch of sweat on each leg. He scanned the field, wondering where Lena was. She seemed so cool, and he felt himself getting aroused at the thought that he would finally, maybe, get to kiss a girl. He squirmed as he felt his hardness rub against the aquablade material of his swimming suit. A broad smile spread across his face. This would show his mates. They were always bragging about the girls that they had felt up, that they had snogged.

But he had actually pulled a girl from Year 11. How cool was this going to make him? He would be a god amongst boys. They wouldn't dare call him gay after this!

"Anthony?"

The boy turned at the sound of a woman's voice. He saw a tall, blonde haired woman striding towards him.

"Miss Yates? What are you doing here?" Anthony wondered why his gym teacher was in the park.

"Be quiet," she said, taking his hand. He tried to pull away, but the thirty-year-old teacher was too strong. She pulled the boy into the dense copse of trees and pushed him to the ground.

Lena picked up the small blue speedos and wiped the blood from the knife as she looked down at the naked body of the young schoolboy. Leaning down, she wiped the trickle of blood from his mouth were she had forced his penis into his mouth. Her sadistic lust and desire were sated for now. She knew that she would need to move once again. People always hated when a child had been mutilated and murdered, and she didn't need that type of attention.

"Sheffield next, I think," she smiled as she walked back to the path. Youthful laughter and a playful bark distracted her for a moment as she saw a teenage boy playing with a puppy. Glancing around, she saw no sign of a parent.

"Oh... hello Miss Yates."

"Hello Jonathan. Where are your parents?"

"At home. I've just brought Buster out for some exercise."

"Well, maybe I can have a little more fun before I go," she thought to herself as she led the boy into the woods. Her mission to gain revenge on boys was going perfectly according to plan.

Mr. Thornton is Quite Frightfully Dead

By

S.J. Gibbs

What will Lena discover in the library?

Lena was raised on violin lessons and minimal parental supervision.

That was how it was that she was to be the one to discover the corpse of Mr. Thornton, her parents always so busy living their own lives often out of town, as they were on this occasion.

She sighed deeply, how inconvenient for the old butler to have died whilst they were away.

Her face flushed and her eyes bright, she ran off in search of Cook or the housekeeper or her governess.

But the first person she came across was Mikey, the stable boy.

"What are you doing inside the house?" she asked him.

"Oh sorry Miss! Cook asked me to get some herbs from the garden, I'm just taking them down to the kitchen."

"Well, more importantly can you ask her to come to the library? I'm afraid poor old Mr. Thornton is quite frightfully dead in there."

His smile faded and his expression became ardent, "Oh my! I'll fetch her at once, Miss."

Cook greeted him with the shake of a fist, "What's took you so long, boy? I'll never have dinner ready at this rate."

Mikey closed his eyes, not wanting t watch her reaction, "I'm sorry but Miss Lena needs you in the library. Mr. Thornton's dead in there!"

"Oh my God! How does she know he'd dead?" She asked wiping her hands on her apron before removing it.

Mikey couldn't help but notice that Cook looked bigger every time he saw her, "I don't know, she just said to get you as quickly as I could."

She rushed as hastily as her size would allow her to up the stairs with Mikey following closely behind towards the library and finding Miss Lena, she asked, "Now, what's all this nonsense? The old fool's probably fell asleep in an armchair. Where is he?"

Entering the library, she saw Mr. Thornton spread out on the floor and on close examination, she declared, "Oh my goodness, he is most certainly dead."

Her voice grew livelier, "Oh why would it happen when your parents were away Miss Lena. Mikey fetch me a phone, we will need to summons the doctor. Miss Lena can you go and find the housekeeper and your governess. Where is she anyway, why isn't she supervising your lessons?"

They all grouped together outside the library and waited 90 minutes for the doctor to arrive, which felt more like 900 to Lena. Nobody seemed to know what to do other than wait and make exclamations about how awful it all was.

Dr. Hilton arrived and greeted Lena with a hug. He'd been a friend of her father's for years. "Well, what have we then, let's take a closer look at the poor old fella."

Lena observed as he stood over the body of Mr. Thornton, "Well, why has nobody called the police. This is quite obviously not a natural death. How could none of you have seen the blood? The poor man's been stabbed to death."

"Don't touch a thing," he shouted at them all. "Not until the police arrive, and none of you are to leave. Do you understand?" he called out in a tone only used by persons who are certain those they call will rush to obey.

Everything became a blur to Lena. A murder had taken place here in her home. She looked around at all the others. Who could have killed poor old Mr. Thornton?

She started to think. She'd seen the housekeeper rowing with him yesterday, but then that was nothing new, they were always at each other's throats, but not literally.

What would her father say? A murder in his household, it would go so against the honor and pride that he liked them all to know ran in his family from previous generations.

Shivering she suddenly felt scared, what if it was her governess? Cook was right, why had she not made her do any lessons at all this morning and where had she been?

Terror ran through her at the thought. She wished now that the police would hurry up and arrive. Why hadn't she thought to call them herself when she'd seen the blood?

A couple of minutes later, a knock at the front door signaled the arrival of two detectives.

Lena heard them ask Dr. Hilton if he was able to pinpoint the time of death.

Exerting his authority, he replied," I'd say he's been dead for at least six hours."

Feeling a bitter taste in her mouth, Lena began to work out what time that would have been. It was now just after 1 'o' clock so that meant it must have happened prior to 7 'o'clock in the morning, when apart from Cook and Mikey the rest of the household would have been asleep.

After establishing everyone's roles within the household, one of the detectives turned to Lena and asked, "Where are your parents?"

"Oh, they're away," she replied.

"Well, they should be notified of what's happened here."

The governess stepped in. "Oh yes! I'll do that right away," she said tucking in a stray lock of hair that had become disarranged.

"Now if I can ask you all to return to your normal daily duties, we will be coming to speak with you all individually."

As they all departed, Lena felt a little deserted. She had no idea what to do with herself or where to go. She'd gone to the library to choose a book to read and obviously that hadn't gone quite to plan.

Something but she wasn't sure what was eating at her conscience. Something about her governess had never sat right with her. There was something about her that she felt was off about her. Maybe she would sneak to her room and have a little nose around. What was the bigger picture with her? Had Mr. Thornton found out something about her that she was afraid he would tell?

It was a terrible ordeal for them all, but Lena was determined to do some digging until she discovered the truth of who had committed this terrible crime.

Lena peeked her curly blonde head around the door to the governess's room cautiously and then entered once she'd established it was empty.

Either situation might be the case, she could be innocent, or Lena may find something in here to prove her guilt.

Actually, she knew very little about her governess who had only been employed by her father since the summer, a few months ago.

The room was clean and airy she noted as she started to look around.

Fear overtook her as she moved from place to place disturbing her governess's belongings.

She hadn't been particularly good at her job. Lena was aware as whenever her parents were away she hardly made her do any of her studies.

The controlled voice of her governess made her jump, "Miss Lena, what are you doing in my room? Have you been rummaging through my drawers? What on earth are you hoping to find?"

"Oh! Sorry. I was just looking for my kitten. I can't find her anywhere," she lied.

"Sweet Miss Lena, with your strong, brave spirit and your pure generous nature, you make a terrible liar. Your performance wouldn't earn you critical acclaim as an actress. Perhaps we should have some drama lessons added to your daily studies."

Scared now, Lena inched further into the corner of the room.

"Don't try and place me in harm's way Lena, else you might find some harm happens to you."

Lena paused for a moment before she probed, "Did you kill Mr. Thornton?"

The evil smile that stretched across the governess's face told Lena everything she needed to know. Now all she had to do was prove it.

JAMS Publishing

Assignment Fifty Three – So all of it was just a lie

16th April 2021

J.M.'s piece was based on a true story that she heard whilst out in Barbados, regarding a man lured to the island by a woman, only to find out that she was already married. The group agreed that the description was exceptional, as always with J.M.

Michael revisited a previous homework, following up the neighbour mail assignment from the very first Words Don't Come Easy with the scene showing the aftermath of the revelation. For once, Michael concentrated on dialogue, rather than scene building.

S.J. wrote another divisive piece, splitting the opinions of the group. J.M. particularly found "his mouth munching at her breasts" hilarious which had not been the intent. S.J. enjoyed exploring a fantasy genre.

Love and Lies

By

J.M. McKenzie

Paul thought Shondelle loved him. He'd changed his whole life for her. How could he have got things so wrong? Or had he?

"So, all of it was just a lie?" said Paul.

"Well," Shondelle mumbled, looking at her hands, which kneaded an invisible ball of dough in her lap. "Not exactly a *lie*."

"Well, it doesn't matter now," said Paul. "It's too late."

"I'm sorry, "Shondelle said. "It's not too late. Please. We can fix this."

She looked sorry, Paul thought. The bright brown eyes that had once gazed lovingly into his, now downcast and shimmering with tears. The full pink lips, that had once kissed his own with such warm desire, were unsmiling and set. She looked genuinely anguished. But then again, was there anything genuine about this woman? Anything at all? He seriously doubted it.

For him, it had been love at first sight. He thought it had been for her too. He was in a bar on the west coast of the island, already on his fourth Rum Sour, and the sun had barely set. Those still in the water, or strolling on the beach, were dark silhouettes against a darkening sky, its clouds washed with a million shades of red and gold. The bar was full of ex-pats and tourists, laughing and chatting as they made the most of the sundowner happy hour. The smell of freshly cooked fishcakes drifted in from the kitchen. He sat alone at the counter on a high stool.

With two messy divorces behind him, and his current relationship back home heading the same way, he wasn't looking for love. He wasn't looking for anything, except his next drink and a couple of weeks of solitary sun, sea and sand. Then, *she* had walked in. Tall, poised and elegant in a flimsy shell-pink sarong that clung her smooth brown curves in all the right places. His wasn't the only head that turned as she walked over to the bar. She climbed gracefully onto the stool next to him and ordered a mango daiquiri. Before he knew it, the words were out.

"Let me get that for you, Darling?"

Of course, she'd accepted and the rest, as they say, was history. He'd been surprised how effortless it was. Especially, as she was way out of his league. But, at 47, he wasn't bad looking for his age. He still worked out and, in between trips to the Caribbean, kept his tan topped up on the sunbed. He kept his silver-grey hair and beard short and trim and made the most of his "piercing" blue eyes (his second wife had told him they made him irresistible to women). His strategy was to wear dark glasses as he was reeling them in, and then, when bringing them up for landing, he'd push the glasses onto his forehead and stare deeply into their eyes. It worked every time.

But he hadn't needed to do any of that with her. He hadn't even been wearing his sunglasses. That's why he'd thought that this time, it was the real thing. It had all been so easy. So natural. This time it was love. He was sure of it.

He knew it that first night. As they made love with the cool sea breeze from the open shutters drying the perspiration on their skin. As her body glistened like tempered chocolate against the white cotton sheets. As she writhed and moaned in ecstasy at his touch. As he opened his eyes in the last spasms of orgasm, and looked into hers, deep and dark with passion. As they lay together in the afterglow, a tangle of limbs, dark and light. He knew that this time it was forever.

And so, it had seemed, it was. Until today.

He'd gone home and tied up the loose ends with his current partner. Then, it had taken him just over a year to sort out his affairs. It had felt like a long time to be apart, but he'd paid for her to come out to him a couple of times and he'd gone back out to see her on a few more occasions. Money wasn't an issue for him. Never had been. That had been part of the problem. Too many gold-diggers. But Shondelle was different. She wasn't interested in his money. She hadn't known anything about him when she'd walked into that bar. She was only interested in *him*.

She'd been surprised when she'd found out about his wealth. Almost uncomfortable with it. Concerned. But he'd talked her around. Reassured her. And, after he'd taken her on her first shopping trip to Mayfair, and she was trying on her purchases back in his Park Lane apartment, the look on her face as she'd twisted and turned in front of the mirror, told him it wasn't going to be an issue.

He sold all his properties except the apartment. Shondelle had said it might be nice for him to keep it, in case they ever fancied coming back to London. He thought she was probably right. He bought a remote clifftop beach house on the east coast of the island, as Shondelle said "away from all the hustle and bustle". A beach house with seven bedrooms, a freshwater and a saltwater pool, and an indoor and outdoor kitchen, mind you. Shondelle had thought they should have somewhere big enough for any of his friends and family to stay, if they wanted to come and visit. Again, she was right. His original idea of a little love nest just for the two of them wasn't really very practical. She was so considerate. She knew what it meant for him to leave his life in the UK for her.

He sold a couple of his businesses and moved the others out to the Caribbean, opening an office in the only settlement on the island that could be loosely described as a "town" (although the locals referred to it as 'the city'). He had wanted to sell them all. He'd been planning to retire at 50 anyway. He would just be bringing it forward by a couple of years. But again, Shondelle had persuaded him not to. She was worried that he might be bored once he settled down to a permanent life on the island. She thought it was important for him to have something to do. She said it would keep him young, be good for his mental health to have some stimulation. Once again, he knew she was right.

And so, he'd finally moved out here. They'd moved into the house and he'd taken a few weeks holiday as they settled in together. It was perfect. They made love in the mornings, breakfasted on fresh fruit and strong coffee on the terrace, then went for long walks on the beach, or cliff top. In the afternoons they lounged by the pool and read or listened to music with their fingers entwined. Shondelle had insisted that they get a cook, so that they could make the most of the time together. She didn't want to waste time in the kitchen on their "honeymoon", as she'd called it. The cook would serve cocktails by the pool at six, and dinner on the terrace at eight. She would clear up and leave them alone again by nine, when they inevitably ended up making love again, but this time outside, on the day bed where the stars twinkled through the mosquito netting, the crickets and tree frogs chirped, and the waves crashed on the beach beneath them.

Paul could have carried on like that that forever, but the time came when he had to go back to work, and they settled into a new routine. The island was small, but the roads were terrible. Narrow and twisting and pockmarked with rucks and potholes. Especially on the rugged east coast which received the worst of the summer rains and was beyond the reaches of the government road repair crews. Even the shortest journey seemed to take a lifetime. He'd leave every day at six, at first light, to cross the island to his office, often not returning until well after dark.

He had no idea what Shondelle did while he was gone. She'd decided that she wanted to keep on the cook, and she'd taken on a maid to help with the housework, and a man to look after the garden and clean the pool. There was just so much to do what with "de house bein' so large an' all" she'd said, looking at him dolefully with her big brown eyes.

"Of course," he'd said, kissing her forehead. "Whatever you need."

But he didn't care what she'd been doing all day, because she was always there, waiting for him on the terrace when he got home. Immaculate and fragrant. She'd greet him with a wide, bright smile and a rum and coke. The ice tinkling deliciously in the glass. Sitting him down. Fussing over him. Taking off his shoes and bathing and massaging his hot and dusty feet. Kissing him. Telling him how much she'd missed him. How much she loved him. How lonely she was without him. How she couldn't wait until the weekend when they would have two whole days together.

But, as the days turned into weeks, and the weeks into months, there were little things that began to niggle in the corners of his mind. Why had he never met her family? She'd talked about them. Talked about inviting them over. Talked about going to visit with them. But, whenever they'd come close to actually making plans, something else had come up, or she'd said why didn't they just have a quiet weekend at home together? He'd been working so hard, was so tired, they could see her family another time. What about her friends? She must have friends. But he'd never met any of them either. And what did she do all day. She never talked about it. She had a car but, as far as he knew, she never went anywhere. They even had their groceries delivered.

Last week, he'd come home early. He told himself that it wasn't to spy on her. That it wasn't to catch her out. That it wasn't because he didn't trust her. He loved her, for God's sake. Loved her more than it was possible to love another human being and she loved him back the same way. He knew she did. That was never in question. No-one could fake that ... intensity ... and for so long. It was impossible. No! He just wanted to surprise her. That was all. So, when his last meeting of the day was cancelled, he shut down his computer and left. There were a million things he could have got on with. A million things he could have done. But he just got in his car and left.

He'd got back an hour earlier than usual. It was still light. Her car was in its usual place in the car port. But there was another car in front of it. A small white car, that had seen better days. He stopped a couple of hundred metres from the house. He sat with the engine running. Watching. His didn't know why, but his heart was pounding in his chest. He was about to tell himself to stop being so stupid, it meant nothing, when a man came through the front door. He jumped into the car and sped off in the opposite direction. Paul only caught a glimpse of him, but he was tall, muscular and dark. Actually, he told himself, he looked a bit like Shondelle. Maybe it was her brother? He was sure she'd said she had a brother.

She wasn't on the terrace waiting for him with a cold rum and coke. She wasn't in the kitchen. Or anywhere downstairs. He found her in the bedroom. She'd just got out of the shower. She looked as if she'd been crying. She jumped when he entered the room. Her eyes opening wide. Her mouth forming a silent 'O'. Her arms clutching the towel tightly around her.

"Paul!" she said. "You make me jump! You early."

"Are you ok? You look as if you've been crying."

"Oh, I fine. Just soap in my eyes. I just getting ready for you to come home. What a lovely surprise."

"Well, get dressed and meet me downstairs. My turn to fix the drinks tonight."

She smiled. "I be five minutes."

He headed for the door, but turned back and asked, as casually as he could.

"Who was the guy in the white car?"

"Oh, that was Michael," she replied quickly. Her voice didn't falter.

"Michael?"

"Yes, he sometime come to help the gardener."

"Oh, ok. Do we pay him extra?"

"Only a few dollars. Cash in hand. He only come occasionally when there be some heavy lifting to do. Sorry, I should have ask first."

"No. I'm sorry! Of course, you shouldn't have to ask. See you downstairs in five." He blew her a kiss.

He told himself it was nothing. He was being paranoid. Overreacting. It had happened before in his past relationships. His jealousy. His suspicion. Eating him up. Spoiling things. He wasn't going to let it happen again.

But, two days later, he'd come home early again. The white car was on the drive. He'd gone straight upstairs. The maid scuttled past him on the stairs. Head down. Avoiding his eye. The bedroom door was ajar. Raised voices from within. A man's voice. Angry. And Shondelle's. Quieter. Pleading.

"Give me more time," she was saying. "I need more time."

"You had all da time!" the man shouted.

Through the crack in the door, he saw Michael, the "gardener's assistant", pacing back and forth.

"But I need *more*. Please." Shondelle begged him.

"You me wife, Shondelle! You sleep here wid him every night! Enough! No more time!"

Paul staggered back as if he had been struck. *His wife?* At the same, time the door burst open, concealing him behind it, and Michael stormed downstairs. Paul waited until he heard the car speed off, before he crept into the next-door guest suite and lay down on the bed. He couldn't think. Couldn't feel. He was numb. He stared at the ceiling, watching the fan spin slowly, listening to the slow thump of its blades as they caressed him with soft cool air.

Later, when he heard her go downstairs, he went into their room. He went through to the ensuite and stared at himself in the bathroom mirror. His tanned skin had taken on a sallow yellowish tone. His evening stubble looked like a dusting of ash on his skin. Small beads of sweat dotted his forehead. The laughter lines around his eyes and mouth looked like deep, dark crevasses. His whole body ached. He looked like an old man.

He poured himself a glass of water and opened the bathroom cabinet. He was sure Shondelle had some painkillers in there. She took them for her period pains. Once, when he'd gone to take a couple for a headache, she'd made a point of telling him how strong they were that she got them on prescription, and that he should get the ordinary paracetamol from the kitchen cabinet.

It was late by the time she came back upstairs.

She was beside herself.

"It's not what you think, Paul!" she was saying now. "Yes, it started out like that, but then I fell in love with you. I really did. I really do. I love you, Paul. I'm so sorry. *So* sorry""

"It's too late, Shondelle," Paul said.

"No, it's not too late. I've been trying to break up with Michael these last few weeks. He's been making it difficult for me. But now that you know, we can sort it out together, Paul! It's for the best that you found out. You can help me!"

"Oh, Shondelle," Paul groaned. "What have you done? What have *I* done?"

"I know! I know! But you can forgive me. I love you. You love me. We can fix this!"

Suddenly, Paul was finding it difficult to speak. "Iss too late, Shondelle," he slurred.

The pills were beginning to take effect. He felt sick. Dizzy.

"Paul, what's wrong?"

He knew something was wrong, but he couldn't think what it was.

"Paul?"

He knew he'd done something, something stupid, but he couldn't remember what it was.

"Paul!"

He was terribly, terribly tired. He lay back on the bed.

Shondelle was crying now. Big racking sobs.

Paul couldn't make sense of what she was saying. Her face was floating in front of his.

"But I love you!" she wailed. "I really do!"

He could hardly hear her now. It was as if she was at the end of a very long tunnel. He could barely see her. It was getting dark. Very, very dark.

"Paul! Paul!"

Paul closed his eyes.

The Loving Lie

By

Michael Andrews

After opening his neighbour's mail, fourteen-year-old Danny Jacobs confronts the hidden truths of his life, and the people who have kept those truths from him.

Jessica sat on the sofa, trying to comfort the boy that she had taken in, the boy she had raised as her own as he struggled through emotions that were raw. She stroked his bare back; in his rush to confront the man next door, Danny hadn't put his shirt back on. She felt his shivers as his sobs became less.

The man, their neighbour for the last three years, watched with nerves evident as their whole world had come crashing down. But maybe this was a good thing, Jessica mused. She had recognised him immediately of course, how could she not? It was HIM. The boy who had stolen her niece's virginity at prom. The one who had gotten her niece pregnant. The one who the family agreed would not ruin that girl's life.

She glared across the room at him. "How did he find out?"

"My mail got delivered to you by mistake," Daniel said softly. "This was in it."

He handed her the letter that Danny had opened. "It was the reply from my solicitor looking into Danny's adoption."

"Why? Why now after all this time?"

Danny sat up, letting go of the hug. This was important, he knew. "Yeah, why now? I thought that my Dad had never wanted me and left when I was born."

"Well, that's true in a way," Daniel sighed. "I was dating your mother, erm... your birth mother, Jessica's niece, in High School and well, I guess, at prom, things went a little further than normal. The next week, she broke up with me, telling me that her family had found out, and I was heartbroken. I tried to change her mind but was told in no uncertain terms to leave her alone."

"That would have been Jack, my brother-in-law," Jessica sighed. "He was very straitlaced and sex outside marriage was a strict no-no."

"Ew! Sex talk!" Danny faked a vomit heave, and the tension in the room was broken.

"Danny," Daniel stared wondering the best way to approach the subject. "I swear to you that I did not know that Gabrielle was pregnant. I was offered a football scholarship in Chicago and left to pursue my dream."

"You were quite the running back, if I remember correctly," Jessica mused. "What happened? Why aren't we watching you on tv?"

"My second year I was hit by a drunk driver and my leg was busted in seven places." Daniel sighed, thinking back about how his life could have been so different. "I moved back home, started working with my Dad and tried to look up Gabrielle, but your whole family had moved."

"Wait..." Danny had a realisation. "My own mother didn't want me either?" He wiped away fresh tears. "What was wrong with me?"

"It wasn't that, son," Jessica said. "Gabrielle was only sixteen and in no place to become a mother. We discussed it and I adopted you. I wasn't able to have my own children, but I love you like you are my own son."

"He is your son," Daniel interrupted. "You have raised him from birth. My private investigator found that instead of giving Danny away like your brother-in-law wanted to, you took him in. You haven't spoken to him ever since."

"They cut me off," Jessica shrugged. "But I had something more precious than money."

"Is this why we've always struggled with money?"

"I wouldn't change it for the world." She patted his leg before he hugged her.

Daniel watched as the obvious love that the pair shared shone through and his initial plan of challenging the adoption to get custody of his boy disappeared in that instant. A new plan formed quickly, speed of thought being one of his main strengths and why he now ran his father's business and had seen exponential growth.

"I want to be part of Danny's life, as his father," Daniel started and seeing Jessica stiffen, quickly moved on. "However, you are his mother and I have no intention of challenging to take him away from you."

"What do you suggest?"

"I've got a home, back in San Jose. It's far too big for me, really, being on my own. Why don't you come and live with me?"

"Are you proposing to me?" Jessica giggled. "I'm a little old in the tooth to be getting a toy boy."

"Like... Ew! Again!" Danny put a finger in his mouth and rolled over, but his mind was expanding with ideas and hope.

"Of course not," Daniel chuckled. "But the house has eight bedrooms, and I can easily get my crew to convert one side into a full suite so that you have your own space. But it would mean that Danny is with me as well as with you."

"San Jose, you say?" Jessica asked and saw the hope in her son's eyes, and the obvious love that Daniel was showing in his. "I much prefer the weather on the West Coast anyway."

Betrothed to the King

By

S.J.Gibbs

Betrothed to the king, but will they ever marry?

"So, all of it was just a lie."

Corina told her wonderful story to the king; but the king would not believe her.

"Let's start again, only this time with the truth," he said. "Is there one of you in particular you think might have been responsible for my brother's murder?"

She dared to glance up at the king, as someone knocked at the door, and she waited for his eruption, as his eyes searched to see who entered his chambers.

His anger was growing; he was becoming more and more impatient.

There would be no point arguing with him, he hadn't believed her story.

Her forthcoming marriage to him was now under serious question.

The archbishop entered and swooped a low bow before his approach.

The king's voice boomed like thunder, "What is it that can't wait?"

Corina smiled to herself, this was a good distraction, to give her time to think.

"I'm sorry, I just came by to see if you needed my help today," the archbishop said.

The king ran his hand across his forehead, "If I'd have needed help I would have sent for you. Now go!"

He turned to Corina, "Now let's get back to the matter in hand."

She wished she could conceal herself in the deep, rich, dark brown hues of the chamber and not stand here before him as though under a spotlight.

The king's brother had not been her friend and had been apparently opposed to their upcoming marriage, prior to his death.

"You must be tired, should I allow you to rest for awhile?" she asked.

"I don't want rest, I want to know who attacked and took the life of my brother. I'm disappointed in you that you have so obviously lied to me. Who and what are you trying to protect from me?"

His words stung her and she felt as though a million cells died within her body.

Corina had been betrothed to the king since her childhood, which to be fair she had not long grown out of.

A fire seemed to snap within her, and her face flushed, "I honestly believe he was drunk and fell into the pond and drowned. I don't believe he was attacked by anybody."

The king's dark eyes set off caution bells within her again.

"So you honestly want me to believe that through his drinking he caused his own last breath?"

"You can carry on trying to dig up information but it will only keep coming around to the same truth. Whoever left you the notelet, stating he had been murdered and that I was somehow involved is a liar."

He rose, held her hand, and led her to the looking glass, "You see that young face is very beautiful, but if I ever discover you have lied to me, it won't stay attractive for very long."

She could take his breath on her neck, she felt sick to her stomach.

"I know your brother's death hasn't been easy for you, it hasn't for me either."

The burial took place, the Friday following. Corina stood quietly beside the king.

Lightning flashed around them and thunder rumbled.

The guards moved to one side as he moved away, Corina following in his step.

With a note of sadness in his voice, he turned to her and said, "I need wine and I need you."

Troubled, she toyed with the necklace around her throat. What did he mean he needed her? If he wanted a woman to please him he summoned one, he had promised he wouldn't take her until their wedding night.

Once back inside the interior of the castle, he said, "Let's go to the bathing pool. We will drink wine there."

It wasn't a question she noted, but a flat statement.

She swallowed down a reply.

Wine was brought and Corina accepted the glass, which was handed to her by the servant.

"Now, let me watch you undress," the king said as he relaxed in the bathing pool, Corina having averted her own eyes as he'd undressed and slipped into the water naked.

"No apologies, no regrets, three months more to wait for you feels like an eternity. I want to take you now; on the day I buried my brother."

Feeling sad, she began to slowly undress, almost child-like as the overweight king watched.

"Hurry, I'm craving for you," he said.

She lifted her chin, meeting his amused gaze defiantly, wishing the castle would collapse around her.

As she lowered herself into the pool beside him, he grabbed at her, his mouth munching at her breasts; the storm was getting closer faster than she'd anticipated.

She gasped and then realized the sound came from her own throat.

He placed a finger to her lips.

Nodding, she choked back tears, as the animal within him rose.

"You are of outstanding beauty. How does it feel to be in the arms of a king?" he asked.

With an air of innocence, she forced herself to smile," It's wonderful."

"We will spend all night together. Touch me," he moved her hand to his penis.

"See I'm in the mood for sex all night long. You will share my bed," he continued.

He bit at her nipple; "I'm ravenous for you."

A pause, before he took another bite at her other nipple.

"I feel as though we should have some assistance here," he turned and banged the gong by the edge of the pool. A manservant appeared immediately. "Fetch three more of my women," he ordered.

"I'll fetch them at once," he replied.

"Maybe we'll make the night turn into a pleasant weekend," the king said.

"Bring some musicians as well," he shouted.

Corina's cheeks flushed even deeper.

"Bring food and more wine," he yelled.

She'd had complete faith that her parents agreeing to the betrothal when she'd been just a child had been the right thing, but now she knew just how wrong they'd been.

The manservant returned with three women, men arrived with musical instruments and female servants carried silver platters of food. Wine was poured again for the king and each of the threesome.

The women were all dressed in white luxurious gowns. Corina ducked further under the water even more aware of her own nakedness.

"Call one of the women over, you choose which one first. She'll pleasure both of us."

Corina leaned back so she could see the women's faces more clearly.

"They're all very gymnastic. Are you scared, you look scared," he said.

He stood up, his erection in plain sight for all to see. He turned to Corina, "Don't feel shame in this. Wait until you've experienced it, you'll be left wanting more."

"Please can we stop this? I don't want this," she said.

"Perhaps I'm being unfair to you but you see I know you killed my brother."

Corina's future life flashed before her, as she recalled the brief encounter she'd had with the king's brother, when he'd pulled her behind a bush near to the pond and raped her. How she'd fought for her own life as she'd pushed him into the pond and and then held his head underneath the water until he'd stopped moving.

She screamed, "He raped me! I didn't intend to kill him!"

"Exactly my dear, soiled goods. You're no different to my other women, and you'll be treated the same."

Assignment Fifty Four - Paul Fischer was a graduate student studying biochemistry at Oxford when he met my mother.

18th May 2021

J.M. had a great deal of fun, exploring the sexual mindset of a teenage boy. Inspired by the television programme Sex Education, it manages to describe the self-discovery of the boy without it coming across as sleazy. The title won the best in book category.

Michael went back to his paranormal routes, with a story about a secret Government project. As he was back into his comfort zone, the group agreed this was perhaps his best piece in this volume.

S.J. wrote a dark tale about love and betrayal while trapped in a cabin, and an unexpected twist for an ending. SPOILER ALERT – S.J. has developed a reputation amongst the group that when she feels it is time to finish the story, a death is sure to follow.

"O" is for orgasm.

By

J.M. McKenzie

Kevin is bored with his unsuccessful attempts to awaken his youthful sexual desires. Maybe dinner with his mother and her mystery guest will prove to be more interesting?

Paul Fischer was a graduate student studying microbiology at Oxford when he met my mother. He must have made quite an impression on her, as she invited him home to dinner that very night.

When they burst into the silence of the big empty house, in a flurry of laughter and chat, wet umbrellas and outdoor coat and shoe removal, I was lying on my bed, eyes closed, thinking (as usual) about Jennifer Albright's budding breasts. I wasn't an expert on the subject, but I was forming the opinion that she probably needed to start wearing a bra. Not that her breasts were big enough to require containment as such, but largely to stop her nipples from poking through the fabric of her pale lilac school blouse. It was very disconcerting. *How was I supposed to focus on my chemical equations and cell structure with them looking at me like that?*

I was not unaware that the breasts, and particularly the poking nipples, should evoke some sort of reaction in me. I knew that thinking about them should make me want to touch myself, and stroke and squeeze myself, until I erupted in some sort of uncontrollable and delightful (but dirty), wet explosion. I knew that's what *should* be happening, but I was acutely aware that thinking about

Jennifer Albright's budding breasts was provoking absolutely no reaction in me whatsoever. I stopped massaging myself. I was as flaccid and still as I had been fifteen minutes ago. Not even a tingle.

Apart from thinking that she might need a bra (*How much were bras anyway?*), and wondering what size she would be and how many she would need (*Were they like pants? Did you need one for every day of the week*?), my mind kept drifting to what we were having for dinner, and when. I was hungry. Mum was late and there was nothing cooking in the kitchen yet. Not as far as I could tell anyway. She sometimes put something in the slow cooker, and sometimes the oven, which she would set to come on automatically, but if she'd done that, the smell would have started to waft upstairs by now.

So, curiosity about who she had brought home with her this time, and the desire to find out what we would be eating and when, was far more compelling than trying to get excited at the thought of Jennifer Albright's breasts. I tucked my flaccid self back inside my pants, opened my eyes, and sat up on the edge of my bed. I glanced around the room to see how it would look to if Mum decided to make an unplanned inspection, as she often did. I sought out my least dirty trousers, from the pile of crumpled clothes on the floor, and put them on, cramming the rest of the garments into the, already overflowing, laundry basket. I gathered up a handful of chocolate wrappers and empty crisp packets from various surfaces and stuffed them into the wastebasket then picked up as many dirty plates and mugs as I could carry, before pushing the rest under the bed. I spread out my textbooks on my desk to look as if I had been working.

I looked around again.

There," I said. "much better."

And headed downstairs.

The greasy, vinegary smell of chip shop chips hit me as soon as I reached the bottom of the stairs. I could hear my mother unwrapping the paper parcels in the kitchen. I took the dirty dishes in and put them on the counter.

"Kevin," she said cheerfully. "Fish and chips tonight I'm afraid. Go into the dining room. There's someone I want you to meet. I'll be through in a minute with the food."

In the dining room, Paul was standing with his back to me, examining my mothers' latest acquisition, a print called simply, *Self Portrait.* It was a view of the artists buttocks from behind, a plain pink image with a tiny notch at the bottom where her thighs began. Paul spun around as I entered.

"Ah, you must be Kevin! Your mother has told me so much about you!"

I was struck dumb. Paul was possibly the most beautiful man I had ever seen. Actually, the *only* beautiful man I had ever seen. I'd never even thought of a man as being beautiful before, didn't even think it was possible, but Paul was. Tall and narrow-hipped in dark jeans and a loose-fitting, white cotton shirt. Sleeves rolled up casually to reveal smooth muscular, lightly tanned forearms. Twinkling blue eyes. A mop of curly blond hair. A wide white smile.

He turned back to the print.

"It's an amazing piece, isn't it?" he said. "So simple, yet so complex, so intimate, so revealing, so ... erotic. Your mother has such exquisite taste."

I hadn't taken much notice of the print before, but now, it made me cringe with embarrassment. He was right. It was ... intimate. I felt my face colour and looked away quickly.

"I'm not sure that fish and ships counts as exquisite taste," I muttered.

He roared with laughter. It pleased me that I had managed to amuse him. I felt myself colouring even more.

"I'll set the table," I said. Fumbling in the drawers of the dresser for napkins, table mats and cutlery. My hands were trembling. What was wrong with me?

"Let me help you with that," said Paul. Taking some of the cutlery from my hands. As he did so, his fingers brushed mine. I felt a wave of electricity pass through me. The hairs on my arms and the back of my neck prickled and I felt a strange tingle in my lower abdomen. For a moment, my throat tightened in something that was almost, but not quite, like the feeling you got before you were going to be sick. I felt a quiver in my groin.

My mother hurried in, juggling three steaming plates of chips and battered fish. The pieces of fish were balanced on piles of chips and rocked precariously when she banged the plates down on the table.

"No airs and graces here I'm afraid," she beamed at Paul. "Take us as you find us, I always say."

"No you ... " I started.

"Be a dear and fetch the ketchup from the kitchen, Kev," she interrupted. She shot me a look. I shot her one back. She never called me Kev. She was flirting again. Big time.

When I returned from the kitchen, they were seated at the table. Mum was toying with her chips and Paul was opening a bottle of wine. He was smiling at her and she was looking at him with puppy dog eyes. It was sickening. I sat down. They hardly noticed.

I barely said a word to them over dinner (if that's what you could call it). They barely said a word to me. I didn't mind. I was happy just to watch them. Rather, to watch him. The way he tilted his head to one side when he was listening to her talk, nodding intently, seeming to hang on her every word. The way he sucked the grease and ketchup from his fingers every time he went to take a sip of his wine. The way his lips glistened with moisture after he ran his tongue across them to lick off a grain of salt, or a crumb of batter.

Later, I lay back down on my bed and closed my eyes. I took my flaccid self out of my pants again. I didn't seem as flaccid as I had before. I felt sort of ... heavy ... more solid. I pictured the image of Hugette Caland's soft powder pink buttocks. I felt myself harden slightly. I pictured Paul looking at the buttocks, sucking his fingers, licking his lips. Looking at me. Looking back at the image. I was hard now. Hard and big and swollen. I rubbed myself. I pulled myself. I felt something building inside me. An itch, or was it a tickle. A wave of sensation. Of pleasure, or was it pain. I pulled and rubbed. The wave took control. I went with it. I groaned. I moaned. I sighed.

"Oh!" I said with some surprise.

Protecting the Secret

By

Michael Andrews

Paul Fischer had done great research into biochemistry but did his experiments take a dark turn? The Parliamentary Committee will decide, or will they?

"Paul Fischer was a graduate student studying biochemistry at Oxford when he met my mother. She was one of six volunteers, all pregnant women, all of whom specialists had identified a genetic disorder with their foetuses."

I sat at the table, my attorney by my side. In front of me, the seven members of the Parliamentary Select Committee stared back, hardened faces giving me no hope that I would see any outcome of this investigation that would allow me to have my freedom.

Sweating, I wiped my brow.

"Mr Jefferson," I started. "I know why we are here, and it isn't to find the truth."

"ORDER!" Jack Harrison shouted. His pudgy face was already red with anger. "We are here serving truth, justice..."

"And the American way!" I chuckled. "You should have been in the movies, although we're in England so I'm not sure why you want to quote The Lost Boys?"

"What?" The Member of Parliament for Amersham looked at me blankly.

"Oh really?" I sighed. "It's the greatest vampire movie of all time!"

"We are not here to discuss your choice of movies," Carole Hastings said, placing a calming hand on Mr Harrison's wrist. "We want to know what has led us to this situation and why we, as a Government committee, need to take the necessary actions that are being proposed by our Military Intelligence Agencies."

"You don't need to take any action," I said. "All I ever did was what you wanted."

"I beg your pardon?" Harrison spluttered. "You killed, no, you murdered over fifteen hundred people."

"Yes sir, erm, and no sir."

"You admit it or not?"

"We did kill those people, sir," I said politely, despite the attorney by my side trying to hush me. "But we did not murder them."

"How do you figure that out?"

I saw the spittle dribble down his double chin. I paused, taking stock of the room. Glancing around, I saw that there were several top-ranking military officers present, as well as civil servants. I held the grin from my face. The civil service. The servants of the people. The 'unbiased' workers who keep our Great Britain ticking along.

He was there, of course. Lawrence Fischer, Paul's father. He was the one who had come up with the theory but ultimately, it was his son. Paul, who had seen the project through. I felt the rage start to run through my veins but had to pull it back in. I made eye contact with him, curled my lip up and sneered at him.

He shrank back in his seat.

"So, why are you claiming this is not murder?" Carole Hastings asked.

"How can it be murder if I was on assignment?"

I chuckled as I saw two of the Select Committee members spray their water over the desk, mopping it up with the serviettes that were in place.

"You're saying that you are part of Military Intelligence?" Carole asked, her voice steady.

The bang of the wooden door interrupted my reply. I heard the sound of boots marching up the aisle and a voice from behind me soothed my nerves.

"Child X cannot answer that question on grounds of National Security and any further questioning of Child X will be prosecuted at the highest level, with the charge of treason brought against those."

I sat back, smiling a wide smile at the seven members of the committee, knowing that I was now free of their questions.

"Point of order, sir!" Jack Harrison yelled. "We are not yet done questioning the boy."

"Yes, you are." Brigadier Naysmith strode past me. He placed a document on the table in front of the chairman of the committee. "This is a signed document by Her Majesty releasing Child X into my custody and that all investigations into his activities are now over."

"This is most irregular, Brigadier." Carole stood up; her immaculate Versace suit framed her black, short hair perfectly. "But if it is Her Majesty's wishes, then we must postpone our investigations for the time being and discuss with the Attorney General."

"This is wrong!" Jack Harrison yelled. "I want that boy charged with murder!"

"This hearing is over." Committee Chairman Peter Jefferson rapped his wooden hammer on the anvil and the seven members stood.

I could feel the hatred from Harrison, and I licked my lip as I stood. The hand of the Brigadier rested on my shoulder. I turned and looked up at him. His expression was fatherly, even though he was not mine, obviously. I had no idea who my father was. None of us did.

"Let's go," he said simply.

I followed him from the building and into the fresh air. Relief washed over me as I saw the blue sky above me, white puffy clouds floating past. I smiled as we walked in silence for a few minutes before he started.

"How did you get caught?" the Brigadier asked.

I immediately looked down at the ground, my shame at failing him washing over me.

"I'm so sorry, sir," I whimpered.

"Stop it," he snapped "You sound like a puppy!"

I steeled myself. "Kenny had been trapped and we had to try to rescue him," I said. "I couldn't leave him behind."

"That's commendable but you know that in certain circumstances, the mission has to take priority."

I could not help the snarl that came from my mouth. I felt a small thrill as I saw the Brigadier take a step back.

"I am the leader of them, and I will not leave anyone behind." I stopped walking, forcing him to take three steps back towards me. "Kenny is my brother, and I could not leave him to die."

"That's commendable and part of the military way, but you are different. Your unit is special."

"I'm sorry, sir," I repeated, and felt a warm glow spread through me as he rubbed my shoulder.

"I know you are, and I am sorry," he said. "I sometimes forget that you're only 13, and that you are all so close."

"Closer than you expected us, sir."

I looked around. We had walked into St James's Park and we sat down by the lake. I kicked off my Nike Air trainers and dangled my feet into the water. I took a long deep breath of the fresh air, away from the traffic of the roads.

"I could like it here, although Scotland would be awesome." I pulled off my shirt, allowing the sun's rays to warm my pale body. "I bet it's really cool up there. The lakes look great."

"You know that can't happen," the Brigadier sighed, putting his arm around me. "You're incredibly special, as are your brothers. We need you to do things."

I grunted. Looking up at him, I could see my deep brown eyes reflecting in his bright blue ones. I leaned into him, feeling the love that I had not felt from anyone, ever since I had been born.

"Do we have to do more stuff?" I asked, hoping the answer would be negative but knowing in my heart that it would not be.

"I'm afraid so," he sighed. "We need to get rid of Jack Harrison. He has become too troublesome. He is looking too deeply into your activities. I want you to take Kenny, as well as Peter with you. It will be another good training exercise for them until they understand what is going on and how they can help to remove our enemies."

"Kenny is sensitive. He doesn't like doing this. I don't want him part of it."

"Take Brandon then," the Brigadier said. "But Kenny needs to come to the game. I can't allow him to compromise you again."

"Is that a threat?" I growled, pushing myself away from him.

"It is whatever you take it as," he replied. "Don't make this a difficult choice."

Brandon, Peter and I gathered in the park, close to Jack Harrison's home. We were all the same age, although I was the oldest by two weeks. We looked at each other, our dark brown eyes linking. As they did, our thoughts became one, as was the link between us thanks to Paul Fischer's work.

"We need to protect Kenny," I muttered.

"He needs to grow a pair," Brandon sniggered.

"He's just taking time to adjust, is all," Peter snapped. "Remember your first time? You pissed all over that woman."

"Shup up" Brandon growled, moving towards Peter.

I sighed and stepped in between them. "Stop it! Both of you. You fucked up Brandon, leaving Kenny alone and that's why we now have to do this."

"He should have killed them women..."

I snarled and raised my hand towards Brandon. He shrank back.

"I'm sorry. It won't happen again."

"Good," I said. "But because of it, we need to get this man and silence him. So, let's get it over with and we can go back home."

"There he is," Peter said, and we all turned, watching Jack Harrison walk slowly into the park. It was a park long known for men of a certain peculiarity to go cruising within, looking for company.

We moved away from the streetlamps and into the small copse of trees.

"Well, let's get naked then," Brandon chuckled, as he peeled off his black t-shirt, showing a firm set of abs.

"Pervert!" Peter giggled back as he unbuckled his jeans, dropping them to expose a pair of blue and red briefs.

"Really?" I said, pushing him to one side. "Superman pants?"

"Hey, they suit me," my brother laughed.

The clouds moved away, exposing the moon. It was only a sliver of a new moon, but that was all we needed. We were not bound by the made-up tales of the legends of man. Paul Fischer's experiments had seen to that. I pulled off my own shirt, ripping the buttons, feeling the ecstasy as my blood started the change. I hated that shirt anyway.

I had barely pulled off my jeans as the first pops of my bones started.

"HHHHHHHHHHHHHOOOOOOOOOOOOOWWWWWWWWWWWWWWLLLLLLLLLLLLLL!!!!!!!!!!!!!!"

The three of us bounded through the woods, seeking our prey. Of course, he had no chance and we feasted on his flesh. I took a particular delight in seeing the recognition in his eyes as he knew that his investigations had uncovered the truth, but no-one would ever know.

We padded back home, our claws scratching loudly on the pavement as we made our way through the quiet London streets. We approached the tall gates of our home, and watched as the four armed guards opened them, watching us warily with their fingers on their gun triggers. I could smell their fear and felt the rush of adrenaline in my blood. I shifted on my haunches and sensed a movement to my left.

No! Back to our rooms! I silently pushed my thought at Brandon, who had taken a step towards them.

He turned slowly but acknowledged my command as the Alpha of our pack.

Brigadier Naysmith was waiting for us and I motioned with my snout for the others to go back to their rooms. I forced my human form into my brain and cried out as my bones and muscles popped and stretched back into my childlike form. He wrapped a blanket around me and helped me back to my feet,

"I wouldn't have believed it, if I hadn't seen it for myself," Carole Hastings muttered stepping forwards. I blushed, knowing that she had seen me naked.

"Ma'am." I nodded at her.

Peter Jefferson smiled. "You see why we need this to be kept secret?"

"Oh yes, Mr Chairman," she said as she approached me and stroked my arm with an almost motherly expression on her face. "We are going to be able to do so much with your pack. Britain will become Great once more."

Sometimes we have to change the course of things for ourselves

By

S.J.Gibbs

Three of us snowed in. What could possibly go wrong?

Paul Fischer was a graduate student studying biochemistry at Oxford when he met my mother.

We'd been snowed in up here for days now, just the three of us.

Can you imagine that? Him twenty-one, me sixteen and my mother thirty-four.

The numbers played on my mind all afternoon.

I was missing my own friends and was feeling in a pretty awful mood.

My mother said the numbers were trivial, but their relationship was making me feel sick to the stomach.

He looks at me with those wondering eyes, and I suspect he isn't sure about me.

I don't want to share my mother with him, and I don't want him to be part of my life either.

My father had built this house in Scotland; we'd lived in it for a while, before the terrible accident that had killed him. Now, we just used it for holidays, our main home being in Oxford.

At the memories of him, I bite my lip and fumble with the ring he gave me on my right pinkie finger.

I study Paul; he's tall, lean and dark. My father was shorter, stouter, and fair-haired.

Since my father's death, my mother is unpredictable; I never know what she might do next. Her latest crazy idea, apart from dating Paul that is, is to shave her head bald.

Paul gives me the creeps, and I suspect he's a lot sharper than he lets on, after all he's a student at Oxford University.

If only my mother understood me better and what she'd putting me through, being stuck here with them.

I take a bite of my sandwich, which my mother has placed in front of me, and almost choke on it as my mother says, "We've some exciting news, Paul and I are getting married. Isn't that just wonderful."

"You're joking right? That makes no sense. You're unstable, you're not thinking properly!"

I watch as with sure graceful movements, she dances around the room, "Oh don't be so jealous darling. You'll fall in love and marry a man one day and then you'll understand.'

"Stop!" I shout. "You're driving me crazy."

This was quickly becoming an argument I didn't want to have.

I search Paul's face with my gaze, hoping to find some sanity registered on it. His response disappoints me. "Your mother's having fun, don't spoil it for her. We are madly in love," he says with a cocky grin.

If only the snow would melt so that we could leave this place. I sigh.

"We're thinking Venice for the wedding. You've always wanted to go there," my mother continues.

There is great uncertainty in my mind in regard to how I'm going to handle anymore time being around them both. "I don't think either of you are being very fair to my feelings, and me" I say.

"Oh we're not being too hard on you. Why can't you just be happy for us?" my mother asks.

"It's all wrong, that's why. Paul is closer in age to me, than he is you. And what are you going to do, pay for everything? He doesn't even have a job!"

"Don't challenge me. You won't win," my mother says. I shrug, feeling as though a cold hand is grasping my stomach and squeezing hard. I smile instead of antagonizing her any further. I rise and take a step forward towards her.

She points her finger and snarls, "Remember I am your mother, you will have respect for me, no matter what."

"Certainly," I reply.

As quiet as a kitten, I leave the room and creep up to my bedroom, the one my father had decorated with love for me. I'd loved this house from the first day I'd come here.

My mother knocks my bedroom door and enters, "C'mon, don't be like this. Come back downstairs and join us."

"I can't stand it. I can't cope with you both flirting with each other constantly."

"You're being so unlike the girl I know and love."

"You're putting me in such a difficult position. How much do you even know about Paul and now you're talking about marrying him."

"It was clumsy of me to drop it on you like that, I'm sorry. I'm asking nothing from you other than to show us both some respect."

My face feels hot, as the realization comes slowly and late, but clear that she really does love him. "I'm sorry too, but I just find him so ignorant and it's immoral that he should sponge off you. He's no money, and no job. My friends find it very strange that a boy of that age should want a serious relationship with somebody your age, especially you having me so close to his age. I can't have a step-dad whose only five years older than me."

"I guess I have just fallen in love. It's not such a crime, is it?"

"I'll try and be more friendly towards him instead of making him my enemy, but promise me you won't rush into marrying him."

My mother's lips remain firmly closed, her eyes glitter, and a wrinkle comes and goes on her pale forehead, and I can't help but notice that she smells of alcohol.

I follow her downstairs, where Pal is waiting for our return. Watching him silently, I do feel there is something strange about him. Under his cap, which he wears constantly even inside the house, his hair looks filthy and matted.

It's late afternoon now and the outside temperature is dropping even lower, the cold is beginning to penetrate inside the house despite the central heating being on full and the open fire blazing.

One of the things I've always loved about the house is its remoteness but now it seems stiflingly isolated and soberly desolate.

The snow is still frozen solid outside and I send up a little prayer that it will begin to thaw very soon.

My mother is in the kitchen now putting every effort into preparing us a good meaty heartwarming stew.

I look at him and it's as if his eyes mock me. I'm convinced my mother's love for him is unrequited and this is causing havoc on my conscience.

We both avert our eyes at the same time, and look down at the floor. It's as though we can read each other's thoughts.

My mother comes through the door from the kitchen, a steaming bowl of stew in her hands. We sit at the dining table and as my mother serves up, he says, "Gosh this looks and smells good. You're the best thing that ever happened to me."

I want to escape from the table but there's nowhere to go without upsetting my mother, so instead I stare at him. She's annoying me too, with all her cleavage on show.

The rest of the evening we sit around doing nothing, which is pretty much all we've done since we arrived here. The snow begins to fall again in a violent storm, causing me to nearly cry. Would there never be any escape? So much for my prayers.

Eventually, I can stand it no longer so I take myself off to bed to read, but the next morning at sunrise the battle within myself about Paul is renewed.

Through the bedroom wall, I can hear him chuckling hoarsely and I imagine him kissing and hugging her.

I hadn't intended to get up so early but I had dozed off when reading the night before and I can't sleep any longer. Grouchy and stressed, I put my hand to the back of my drawer to find my cigarettes and lighter. I go downstairs and stand at the back kitchen door to have a sneaky smoke before they come downstairs, and my thoughts turn to my father's death, which I try not to mourn too sadly for fear of upsetting my mother.

Is Paul just after my mother's wealth? My father had left her considerably well off and then there'd also been a sizeable insurance payout for his accident.

The strain of being snowed-in is wearing on me. I close the door shivering against the cold and after hiding my cigarettes and lighter I move to the sofa and start to read where I'd left off the night before.

Paul comes down first in a pair of jeans and a t-shirt.

"Are you trying to talk your Mum out of marrying me?" he asks.

"Right now, I don't care what either of you do," I say watching him carefully.

A little after noon my mother finally emerges from her bedroom. She leans forward and kisses Paul on his lips. I pause and take a deep breath.

As she turns I notice she's holding a bloody cloth over her nose.

"What's happened to your nose?" I ask.

She crooks her eyebrow, "Just a nose bleed, darling. I'll do us all some brunch, mushrooms, peppers, onions, sausage and cheese. How does that sound?"

Paul arches his long neck and spreads out his bony legs, "UYeah! Sure! Sounds good to me."

Why is it every time he speaks it's as though he's sucking all the energy from the room?

Over brunch we discuss what we should do for the afternoon, but none of us can think of any way to better our position.

I look down at my empty plate as his lips return again to my mother's and linger in a way that makes me feel sick.

"I think that's sufficient enough for me to put my head back in my book," I say as I push my chair back away from the scene unfolding before me.

Thoroughly provoked by their lack of decency, I pen my book but I can't concentrate on the words, as I listen to their feverish moans for one another.

I move to the kitchen and take the largest and sharpest knife I can find. He thinks he is better than me, well I'll show him.

The opportunity is there for the taking. I'll stop him from being so positively rude to me, in a way he never thought possible.

With a slight smile on my face I leave the kitchen and move towards him.

"Good night," I say as I plunge the carving knife straight into his chest.

The blood bursts out from him, like the red wine they've been drinking over brunch. The noise he makes with his mouth sound strange.

I hear the heartbreak in my mother's voice as she rushes to his aid and squeezes her hand over his chest.

"I haven't finished yet," I say as I remove the knife and plunge it back into his chest once more.

As my excitement grows, I stab faster at his flesh.

In my mind time stops.

I am no longer me, I am a character in one of my books, a bodiless demon.

Sometimes we have to change the course of things for ourselves.

The act was done; there was no questioning of whether he was dead or not.

What my mother didn't know, and would never now know was that I'd had a one-night stand with him six months before he'd met her, when I was only fifteen.

He'd gone from child to parent, but he'd never do it again.

JAMS Publishing

Assignment Fifty Five - Matthew had moved since Johnnie's murder

17th June 2021

This was the first of the new assignments that we were setting ourselves.

J.M. wrote a serious piece regarding two little boys fighting over their toys with drastic consequences. It was one of J.M.'s shorter pieces but still contained all the high standards of her writing that we now come to expect.

Michael wrote a piece that split the group, confusing some while enthralling others. His ability to make fantasy believable shone through with a story about the repercussions of a childhood murder.

S.J.'s piece was a story about inescapable guilt that would follow them wherever they went. S.J. was very happy with this piece, entering it into the Henshaw short story competition.

Dungeons and Dragons.

By

J.M. McKenzie

Matthew's friend Johnnie has just been violently murdered. He is still alone at the scene of the crime. Who and where is the murderer? Should he try to flee or stay where he is? Who is thumping about in the room above him?

Matthew had moved since Johnnie's murder. Not a lot, but he *had* moved. When the pool of blood from Johnnie's body had begun to clot in a sticky congealed mess that began to seep between his fingers, he had lifted his hand and placed it in his lap. Other than that, he had remained stock still in the exact position he had had found himself in immediately after the death had occurred. He hadn't looked at Johnnie's body. Hadn't looked at the splatters of blood and gore on the walls and ceiling. He knew he must be covered in it. He had felt the warm wet splashes hit the bare skin of his hands and face. But he couldn't bring himself to look down at his clothes. Couldn't look at any of it. Once he saw it, it would be real. There would be no taking it back. No pretending it hadn't happened. No more space for denial. No. So, all he had done was calmly and quietly moved his hand when the sensation of the cold gelatinousness on his sensitive fingers became more than he could bear.

He was in a cellar. It was lit by a bare bulb that dangled from a fraying cable. There were no windows and just a single door that he knew opened onto a narrow, dark, staircase that led up to the house. The walls were lined with shelving laden with cases of wine, and crates of beer, jars of jams, preserved fruits and pickles, trays of potatoes, carrots and beets, and few gardening tools and equipment. It smelled of earth and blood and fermenting fruit. A handful of Dungeons and Dragons miniatures were scattered on the floor in one corner of the room. Johnnie had been on the verge of trading his *Vadania the Half-Elf Druid* for Matthew's *Displacer Beast* when it had ... happened. Matthew was still clutching *Vadania* in his other, thankfully clean, hand.

Upstairs he could hear someone moving around. Floor boards creaked and adult sized footsteps thudded on the ceiling.

Mathew was terrified. He knew he was in trouble. Serious trouble. As the initial, brain freezing shock of the murder began to fade he started to consider what might happen next. About what he should do. He didn't know whether to stay where he was or try and run. There was nowhere to hide in the cellar. The stairs opened out into the room above and someone was in there. Then, the footsteps from above began to descend the stairs. He began to tremble, and then to shake, with fear. His little heart hammered in his chest and his breath came in shallow panicky gasps. A wet warm feeling spread out inside his pants as his bladder emptied involuntarily.

The door opened and his mother stood in front of him.

She looked at Johnnie and the puddles of blood on the floor. She looked at the red splashes on the walls and ceiling. She screamed and then put a hand over her mouth. She was looking at Matthew's hand, the one that he had moved and that was now was resting in his lap.

Matthew followed her gaze and also looked at his hand, and at the bloodied two-pronged weeding tool clenched in his small fist.

"Matthew!" his mother cried. "What have you done!"

"I'm sorry, Mummy," Matthew wailed. "But I *really* wanted *Vadania the Half-Elf Druid*"

A Journey to Hell

By

Michael Andrews

Matthew had been on the move ever since his brother Johnnie had been murdered as a child. With no one taking responsibility, it falls upon higher powers to ensure that justice is served.

Matthew had moved since Johnnie's murder. His parents thought it was for the best. After all, he was only thirteen years old when it happened, and a young boy should not have to be reminded of such horror that they had walked into. It had been a good home, a family home. But one that had seen the death of the eleven-year-old Johnnie. However, time had not healed the wounds in his heart.

Matthew looked up at his new home and smiled. He could hear birds singing away to each other, the smell of primrose flowers easing his mind as he settled into the rocking chair on the veranda that overlooked the back garden. He tried to ignore the chattering that was coming across from the annoying couple that lived next door, but he knew that in this retirement village, he would have to put up with it.

The bark of a dog awoke him from his slumber, and he shook himself slightly, before rolling up his trousers to let the sunlight work its magic on his pale legs. The sun was warm down here in Texas, unlike the cold climate of North Dakota. Stretching his body into a yawn, the sixty-seven-year-old army vet smiled as he felt the warmth ease the aches and pains of his body.

His hand moved to the scar that ran just underneath his ribcage. The jagged purple scar reminded him of the broken bottle that he regretted ever holding on that fateful day.

"It always hurts when I think about you," Matthew muttered under his breath. He scowled in pain as he reached over to the table by the side of him. Picking up the crystal glass tumbler, he took a smell of the harsh whisky before drinking it down in one swift gulp. Grabbing the bottle, he poured out another measure and held the glass up to the sunlight, marvelling how the golden liquid prismed the light before his eyes.

"Hello there, new neighbour," a cheery voice shouted out.

Matthew looked up and saw a silver haired man holding out two fishing poles.

"Fancy joining me to see if we can get a decent dinner around here?"

"Fuck it, why not," Matthew said to himself. Easing himself out of his chair, he walked slowly to his new neighbour.

"They call me Jay around here," the silver haired man introduced himself, which caused the hairs of Matthew's neck to shiver. "There's a lot of good fish to catch around here, easy if you know the right bait."

"Wait..." Matthew stopped in his tracks. "What do you mean?"

Jay shook the fishing poles. "I mean that the fish are biting, and they cook really well on the barbeque. Something in the air makes them taste real good when they've been cooked over the coals."

"Do I know you?" Matthew asked.

Jay looked at him, a sparkle in his bright blue eyes. "Maybe in another life? I hope that you do not mind, but I prefer to be up front and honest. I'm gay, but don't worry, I'm not trying to hit on you."

Matthew stiffened as the older man let out a chuckle. Jay's smile started to drop from his face.

"I see that I've offended you," he started. "I'm sorry. Maybe I should leave?"

Matthew wiped the sweat from his brow. He glanced up at the sun, which was now beating down with relentless heat.

"No, it's okay," he stuttered. "My brother was gay, and, well, I didn't really handle it very well."

"Sorry to hear that," Jay said, sitting down beside his new companion. He opened his cool bag and pulled out two bottles of Bud. Popping the caps, he handed one to Matthew before taking a long, deep slurp of his own.

Letting out a belch, Jay giggled as if he was a child, which lifted Matthew's mood.

"You remind me a little of him," Matthew started, taking a swig of his own alcohol. He stretched out, letting the heat of the sun warm his aches away. He glanced at his new friend and felt a stirring that he had tried to hide for all of his life.

Jay stretched out in the chair beside him. He had undone his shirt and Matthew could not help but notice the firm six pack that rippled across Jay's body. Matthew felt himself stirring in places that he did not feel comfortable.

"This is wrong!" he said suddenly, pushing himself out of his chair.

"What is?" Jay asked.

"You. Looking like that. Trying to tempt me!" Matthew felt anger flood through him, and he picked up his bottle. Holding it by its neck, he smashed the base against the table and turned on the homosexual that was trying to lead him astray.

"What's wrong Matthew?" Jay asked.

Matthew snarled as he turned towards the man who was trying to lead him astray from God's path. "I'll not let you tempt me into following you to Hell, demon spawn!"

Despite his aches and pains, Matthew covered the four steps in an instant and plunged the broken bottle into the neck of his guest. Jay cried out in pain, his hands holding his neck, trying to stem the flood of blood flowing down his shirt.

"Mattie? Why?"

Matthew looked down and saw the body of his eleven-year-old brother, crying, convulsing as his life blood ebbed from the stab wound in his neck.

"Johnnie?" Mattie cried out, as he dropped the broken bottle and fell to his knees. He ripped off his shirt and pushed it against the deep wound in his younger brother's neck.

"Why did you hate me so much? Just cos I fancied Billy?" Johnnie's voice sounded pitiful, but there was an underlying hatred within. "Why couldn't you accept me?"

"I'm so sorry," Mattie cried. "I didn't know better at the time."

"I hate you!" Johnnie whimpered as a blood bubble burst upon his lips, turning the ruby red into a scarlet trickle of blood. "I hope you rot in Hell."

"Forgive me, please," Mattie cried as the sky around him turned into a deep, dark black. All sound stopped. As he hugged his dead brother's body, the air around him changed. He glanced over his shoulder, before noticing that his body had transformed back into that of his thirteen year old self.

"Mom. Dad. Help me please!" Mattie cried out.

"You are beyond our help," they said in unison. "You deserve this."

A loud cackle echoed around the boy and Mattie looked up and knew terror.

"Your soul is mine until the end of time, and you will suffer for what you have done to your innocent brother. He is in my Father's Silver City, drinking Ambrosia. You are mine to torment for eternity."

Mattie felt his body shudder as he knew fear, he knew dread, he knew he was damned.

"I'm so sorry, Johnnie," he cried out. "I didn't know or understand what it meant."

The thirteen-year-old picked himself up and stared at the Devil. "Do what you must, because I deserve it." Tears streamed down his face as he finally acknowledged that he had been so wrong about his brother and his brother's sexuality.

Lucifer smiled as he raised up his mighty trident, ready to plunge it into the chest of his latest victim. He knew that the pain his trident caused would last for millennia and he was desperate for the latest bigot to be tortured as he deserved.

Mattie stood and waited. He knew that he was damned, and he knew that he deserved it. Closing his eyes, he whispered a silent prayer of forgiveness, not to God but to the brother that he had murdered.

"STOP!"

White light broke through the darkness and warmth enveloped Matthew. The sixty-seven-year-old opened his eyes and, with the sight of the boy before him, he dropped to his knees.

"Johnnie, I'm so sorry," he cried out as the form of his murdered eleven-year-old brother walked towards him. "I know I was wrong, and I tried to make up for it."

The blonde, eleven-year-old boy glanced at his brother before turning towards the Devil himself.

"I've watched him over the last fifty years and Mattie has dedicated himself to helping and supporting LGBTQ causes. He even fostered some kids. That has to count for something?"

"He took a life," Lucifer growled. "My Father's Commandment number six states that he is now damned to Hell and my punishment."

"That's true unless he is forgiven of his sin." Johnnie turned to his brother. Shaking his body, the young boy smiled as two wings of brilliantly pure white feathers erupted from his shoulders. "Oh man, I was hoping I'd get these."

Johnnie's giggles attracted various demons who crawled over towards Lord Lucifer's throne.

"If it is okay with you, my Lord," Johnnie bowed towards the King of Hell. "I'm going to take my brother upstairs."

Lucifer let out a sigh. "Tell my Father that if he wants me to do a proper job down here, then he shouldn't give you lot the way out like he keeps doing."

"It is a good way out though," Johnnie laughed and held out his palm, raised slightly above his head.

"Fine! It is," Lord Lucifer sniggered as he high fived the eleven-year-old. Turning to the sixty-seven-year-old man, his frown spread back across his face. "You got off lucky. If your brother had not shown unconditional love, you would be mine."

Matthew looked lovingly into his brother's eyes. "I know and I will be forever grateful."

"Let's go home," Johnnie said and held out his hand before turning towards a bright light. Matthew gasped as he saw his parents standing in front of him, arm in arm. His heart expanded and he knew love, unconditional love. He felt a warmth spread through his body and he noticed that his elderly frame had reverted to the body of his youth. He turned back towards his brother.

"I love you," Mattie said, and the thirteen-year-old boy felt his younger brother jump into his arms.

"I love you too, Mattie," Johnnie said. "Let's go home."

Johnnie's Murder
By
S.J. Gibbs

Can Matthew find solace after Johnnie's murder?

Matthew had moved since Johnnie's murder.

When his gaze met his wife Florence's, it was bland.

There was no way to prevent episodes of sleepwalking, and ever since they'd moved it had become a real problem.

"Come Matthew, let's get you back to bed," she said.

She didn't miss the way he bristled as turned he back to her and returned to their bedroom.

Florence shivered, the storm outside, turning her cold. Matthew's mental health was failing steadily, she thought listening to her gut feeling about it all.

Her life felt as though it was running in slow motion. He had become a cruel and nasty man.

His birthday was tomorrow, when in fact he would be 40 years old, with very strong emphasis on the word 'old,' she thought. What had happened to the cheery young man, she'd once known and loved?

The winter rain battered the bedroom window. Unable to sleep she entered the study and started up the computer, pulling up a word document, she began to type. Consumed with fury about her situation with Matthew, she banged heavily on the keys on the keyboard, but the anger she felt was making the novel she was writing flow easily, and she embraced it like it was a newborn child, fresh and eager.

Her attention shifted back to Matthew, who was still sleeping. He'd always been able to make her laugh, before they'd moved.

They had to move forward and leave the past behind them, but he seemed incapable of doing so.

She pulled her oversized dressing gown tighter around her, as tears ran down her face. Yes, she did still love him but it was all so difficult. She bit her lips to keep them from quivering and blinked her eyes to get rid of the blur.

The grisly scene they'd attempted to leave in their past surfaced in her mind. The images as vivid as the day it had happened, the day of Johnnie's murder.

They'd rented a cabin in the woods, not only to get away from everything and to find some peace and quiet but also due to the fact it had been cheaper than staying in a hotel.

The day they'd arrived, she'd jumped out of the car shouting, "It's wonderful! So peaceful!"

By the middle of the week they'd relaxed into a routine whereby Matthew spent his days shooting and fishing and Florence took advantage of the solitude to work on her latest novel. They would meet up around 4, open a bottle of wine, prepare dinner and then go for an evening stroll.

"This is bliss, I could live like this forever," Florence said as they walked through the woods on the third beautiful calm evening of their stay.

On their return to the cabin, they opened another bottle of wine and sat together in a hammock, which swung from two solemn trees at a short distance from the hut.

"I'll go and get us some cheese and biscuits," Florence said as she rose from the hammock.

Five minutes later, Matthew heard the scream. Without hesitation, he retrieved his shotgun from the rear boot room of the cabin and entered with it loaded and pointed directly ahead of him. Although there was light from the kitchen, the lounge was in semi-darkness. A figure moved. Matthew fired the gun. A flash of light. A deafening blast. A thud to the floor.

Confusion grabbed him, what had he done? Shock that he had fired the gun overcame him. A cold feeling washed over him with a wave that was staggering.

He snapped on the light switch, "Florence are you okay?" he shouted. A deep furrow ran across his forehead.

She entered from the kitchen, shivering.

"Thank God," Matthew said. "Are you alright?"

Florence dropped the knife she was holding.

They both stared in disbelief at the man lying very obviously dead before them.

"Oh my God! You've shot your brother!" She rushed towards him to feel for a pulse, even though she knew there would not be one. "Johnnie! You've killed Johnnie!"

For a few moments they sat in silence, before Florence grabbed a red blanket from the couch and threw it over him, covering his face.

"I can't bear to look at him," she said.

"Why was he here? Why didn't he tell us he was coming?"

"I knew someone was in here, I knew it wasn't you as I could still see you in the hammock from the kitchen window. That's why I screamed to get your attention."

"But where's his car? I never heard an engine, did you?"

"He must have tried to give us a surprise visit. You know what a joker he can be. Could be," she corrected herself as the words sank in. "I bet he parked it in the distance somewhere, was going to make us jump. He'd think that would be funny, spooking us out. It'll be classed as murder. You'll go to prison forever," she cried.

"But I didn't intend to kill him and I thought he was a n intruder who'd already harmed you," Matthew said twinged with guilt.

"We need to cover it up. Cover up the murder. Nobody will know he's been here. We hide the body and get rid of the car. You can't go o prison. I couldn't cope with it," she said.

With his mind confused and teased, Matthew readily agreed to her suggestion.

"No one knows what the future will hold for us, but if we face this together, we may just get away with it," Florence said.

Matthew stared at her intensely, "I can't believe what I've done."

****

Of course they'd been questioned, but were unable to remember anything of note to the disappearance of Johnnie. As a crime writer, Florence had covered their tracks well.

They'd moved twelve months later, hoping to put the whole ordeal behind them, but it had done nothing but than turn Matthew into an old man, his character flaws becoming increasingly obvious as the months passed, despising himself and Florence for their wickedness. It was amazing how a person could change so much. His world had become a permanent grey.

At breakfast on his 40th birthday his voice sounded mechanical to his own ears, "I can't do this anymore Florence. I need to end it."

She knows he's lost and desperate but if she allows him to turn himself in, she is lost as well, an accessory to a murder.

"That's crazy! You can't do that after all we've been through," she placed a cigarette in the corner of her mouth and lit it with a match.

The encounter was frightening her more than she was able to admit, "You're missing the point here, I would go to prison as well.'

"I guess I really just wanted to say goodbye," he said as he tipped a bottle of tablets into his mouth and took a large gulp of water and swallowed.

Assignment Fifty Six – Once Upon A Time.

6th August 2021

This was the first prompt in this anthology where the group did not like the idea. We totally blame S.J. as it was her prompt!

J.M. wrote a clever twist on a fairy tale, using her expertise to write a condensed short story while keeping the standard high. It was the first time that any of the group explored the topic of the pandemic.

Michael wrote a dark piece, exploring the potential madness of a paranoid man's dreams. This is an expanded piece of a previously written short story and will be featured in his forthcoming collection *Supernatural Shivers.*

S.J. did not enjoy writing this piece, going into fantasy having been given no choice with the prompt. It is a genre that she is not familiar with, and the story ended up a confusing tale.

A Fairy Story.

By

J.M. McKenzie

Once upon a time, long, long ago, in a land far, far away, there was a kingdom where people were free to do whatever their hearts desired.

Once upon a time, long, long ago, in a land far, far away, there was a kingdom where people were free to do whatever their hearts desired.

They could be with whoever they wanted to be with, whenever they wanted, for as long as they wanted, as often as they liked. They could leave their homes as often as they wanted to and go wherever they wanted to, whenever they wanted, as many times as they liked. They could travel back and forth to other lands whenever they felt like it. They could be with as many people as they wanted to all at the same time outdoors or indoors. They could stand close to each other. They could shake hands with each other. They could hug and kiss each other. They could dance and sing and laugh.

They trusted each other. They loved each other. They didn't judge each other. They didn't criticise each other. They weren't fearful of each other. They didn't watch each other. They didn't avoid each other. They didn't hide from each other.

They could go to work and school without fear. They could earn money. They could learn. They could pay their rent and their bills and buy food. They could go shopping and go to pubs and bars and restaurants without fear.

They could celebrate birthdays and weddings and anniversaries with all their friends and families. They could play and watch sport. They could go to shows and plays and concerts. They could go to festivals and carnivals. They could indulge all their interests and be part of clubs and groups and societies.

They could come together to say good bye to loved ones who had passed.

They didn't have to wash their hands and faces all the time. They didn't have to sanitise their skin with harsh chemicals all the time. Thy didn't have to cover their faces with masks. They didn't have to provide their contact details every time they went anywhere. They didn't have to keep far away from each other. They didn't have to have vaccinations.

They didn't demonstrate. They didn't protest. They didn't fight.

They weren't watched. Their movements weren't tracked. They didn't have to be screened and scanned wherever they went. They didn't need tests and vaccine passports. They didn't need self-isolation, and quarantines and curfews and lockdowns.

They didn't get 'pinged'.

They didn't get sick. They didn't die.

They didn't cry.

They weren't lonely. They weren't afraid. They weren't confused. They weren't sad. They didn't go mad.

They weren't angry.

Thy didn't feel guilty, ashamed, or dirty.

Once upon a time, long, long ago, in a land far, far away, there was a kingdom where Covid didn't exist.

Once Upon A Time

By

Michael Andrews

Not all stories that start with those magical four words are fairy tales. Not all princesses are kind. But stories are just stories, made up to keep children happy... or are they?

Once upon a time. That's how all the good stories start, isn't it?

Once upon a time there was a princess locked in a tower who was saved by her knight in shining armour who rode a pure white steed and they lived happily ever after. Blah blah blah. Very nice. Whatever!

However, real-life isn't a fairy tale. Some princesses do not need or want to be saved. I've fallen foul of them ever since I discovered them. Selfish bitches who are looking out only for themselves, who are looking for a man to snare, to suck his soul dry and cast aside the empty shell of his being at the first opportunity.

And then there is the special type of demon princess. The witch. The hag. The one who devalues everything good about you. The one who makes you feel worthless, that everything you have ever done has been a waste of time.

I can still hear her cackly voice echoing in my head. "You're such a loser; you'll never get ahead in life. You will never amount to anything."

Her dark soul seemed to pass from one princess to another, haunting my life wherever I tried to run.

She was there when I was just a young boy. "Dumb kid, stupid boy, idiot child." Those names that woke me each dreadful morning as I climbed from under the safety of my blanket and continued until I was pushed through the front door to start the walk to school. Those names that greeted me when I returned home, trying to be invisible as I ate my dinner alone in silence. Those names that followed me up the stairs to my bed, and it was only underneath my blanket as I closed my eyes and fell into a fitful slumber that the names stopped ringing in my ears.

As I grew older, I started to fight back, to try to be that brave knight, but my body soon learned that it was not just names that hurt, but that sticks and stones really did break bones. I tried to run away on several occasions, looking for my perfect princess to save me, but each time, they returned me to the hag-witch-demon, and my pain increased.

At fourteen, I thought I had finally escaped, ran away, and this time, they could not make me return. She tried to convince them that I was mad, insane, crazy, but I would not back down. I told them about the beatings, but there had been no proof. I showed them the scars where she had cut me with a kitchen knife, but she said that I had done it to myself, that I had episodes, that I was convinced that she wanted to hurt me.

They put me in a nice safe room, my own personal tower, I guess. I had to take a pill each morning. It would help with the voices in my head, they said. They didn't understand that those voices were not imaginary. It was *her* voice. *Her* words. Only now, the words were "Crazy kid, insane idiot, bonkers boy."

The voices would follow me as I slept, as I ate, as I walked around dingy white corridors that smelled of bleach and chlorine. They came out of the mouth of the nurse who watched me as I showered, making sure that I didn't "hurt" myself. They came out of the mouth of the cook who spooned the slop that they called food on to my plate.

Every single princess was that hag, that witch, that demon.

They did not like it when I stabbed the princess who watched me. I had hidden my drawing pencil in my sock when they hadn't been looking. I popped both of her eyes so that she could not watch me anymore. They did not like that at all.

They strapped me in my bed at night, and the voices cackled in my ears, in my brain, "Evil child, dangerous boy, demented kid."

They didn't like it when I worked my right arm loose and stabbed the princess who came in to give me my pill the next morning. I pushed the post of the buckle into her neck. For a moment, the voices stopped laughing at me as I was showered in her red blood that sprayed across my bed before she fell to the ground, and I was strapped up once again, more securely than before.

"Murderous child, dangerous boy, killer kid." The hag's words changed each time.

I would lie awake, seeing her face in front of me—the ever-changing face of the demon princess. Sometimes she looked like my mother, sometimes the girls from my school, and sometimes women I didn't even know.

But their words were all the same.

They gave me more pills, and the voices stopped. I would sit in my chair, spittle and drool dribbling down my chin as my vacant stare took in nothing of my surroundings.

They would inject me with needles and take me on a trolley to a room full of machines. They put me in a long tube and said that they were taking pictures of my brain.

They gave me different pills, and I started to feel better. I could focus. I could see once again. I would sit in a group and talk about my feelings with others. It helped. I was getting better.

I *was* better. The hag-witch-demon princess no longer spoke to me, and I had escaped.

They said it had taken seven years to get better. Seven years of my life that I had lost because of my own imagination. I smiled at them, even as the hint of a dark shadow edged around the corner of my vision. I shook it off. Shook their hands, and started my new life.

They gave me a small self-contained apartment. It was nice, but it was noisy. I would go for walks alone in the park, in solitude, escaping the noise of the chattering princesses from the room below.

It was one of those nights when she came back to me. She was in the princesses that were all around me. Every single princess was shouting at me.

"Evil man, dirty boy, killer kid, stupid boy."

I ran back to the apartment, to the sanctuary of my room.

The door closed quietly behind me. I heard the click of the lock and walked slowly through the hallway. Kicking off my shoes, I dropped my rucksack onto the floor next to the small wooden table onto which I put my keys.

I stared into the silver-framed mirror, not recognising the thin, sallow face that stared back at me. I ran my right hand through my blonde hair, brushing the stray locks of my fringe back into place.

Hanging my coat on the hook, I walked into the lounge, dropping myself onto the black leather couch. I swung my feet up and closed my eyes for a moment. I took in deep, slow breaths as I calmed myself down.

The noise from outside echoed through the room, and I frowned, opened my eyes, and scowled at the open window. The cars and the people from the busy street below would not leave me alone.

I just wanted to be left alone, to be alone.

I held my hands over my ears, but it was no good. The noise was too loud, too much.

Standing, I grabbed the small coffee table and threw it at the window. The shattering of glass was a magnificent sound, but it only made the outside noise so much louder.

Staggering across the room, I bumped into the sideboard, and music blared out. Glancing down, I'd accidentally switched on my stereo, and music, my normal comfort, was now my enemy, invading my peaceful place.

"Headphones!" I gasped. Grabbing them, I put them on, blocking out all sound once I had thrown the stereo across the room.

Silence greeted me once more. My happy place. My silent place.

I was alone once again. I could let my mind go blank. I could shut out the thoughts, those horrible thoughts that threatened to invade my solitary existence.

I closed my eyes to revel in the darkness; the peacefulness of nothing but the face was there again. Her face. Her mouth was open; I could see her smile of joy; I could hear her laughter in my head. I shook my own from side to side, banging my fists against my forehead, but it was no good. Even in darkness and silence, she was following me. She would not leave me alone. She would *never* leave me alone.

My right arm flailed to the side, and I felt it knock over a plastic container. Squinting through narrow eye slits, I saw the bottle of sleeping pills that I had to take just to get a couple of hours respite from the agony of insomnia.

Twisting the cap open, I poured a dozen tablets into my palm and grabbed the half-full glass of water by the side. I threw the pills into my mouth and took a deep gulp of tepid water. I nearly gagged as I felt the fly that I noticed at the last moment hit the back of my throat.

But I swallowed it and the pills before taking a second handful, then a third. By the sixth time that I tipped the bottle, there were just four tablets left. I greedily supped them down and laid back on the sofa, my arms folded over my eyes.

Her face was there again; her laughter filled my ears once more. There was a smugness behind it.

"You've won," I whispered softly to her. "This is what you wanted, isn't it?"

"Dead boy, dead boy, dead boy… come and join me."

Her face seemed to beckon me towards her.

I felt warmth as sleep overcame me.

Everlasting sleep.

And they all lived happily ever after?

By

S.J.Gibbs

Did they all live happily ever after?

Once upon a time Punor was not only impoverished but was broken in spirit as well. The death dealer was always sniffing around, hoping to recruit some more souls to condemn to Hell, but he was no match for Jove the Sorcerer, with his heartless, cruel eyes.

The question for both of them now was who was to win with the soul of Punor, and they were doing their utmost to gain his goodwill.

"I'm not interested in an arrangement with you," Punor said to the death dealer. Jove has offered me wealth and a beautiful house. He's going to make me a successful merchant."

For the death dealer it was a bad day, as he sat in his cave, which was only a narrow hole between two rocks.

"Do you believe Jove's fairy tale fantasy and all of his magic? I can give you eternal life in the beyond. It's a bad decision you're making. This world is overpopulated. I can take you to a world of dreams. I understand the decision is of peculiar delicacy and difficulty but I can offer you so much more than he can. You should consider the special attributes of the anthropomorphic God I can introduce you to. All you have to do is agree. Do you not understand what type of an evil creature Jove is?"

Punor's defense was weak and inapt but he still believed Jove to be the least of two evils, and the promise of wealth and a beautiful house without having to die seemed far the better option.

And so it prevailed that Jove with his big grey eyes and beautiful red hair won the soul of Punor.

The wealth and beautiful house did not materialize and Punor found himself virtually a captive in Jove's domain.

"Suppose we pick the Royal Princess as our next soul," Jove said to Punor as he waved his arms casing the sand on the ground to transform into a mist and swirl around him.

Punor saw the beast before Jove. It was very close to them now. His future flashed before him.

The beast's approach was light almost advancing with levity, before it made its attack, which was carried out with splendid triumph. Jove the Sorcerer fell to the floor, his soul departed his human form.

Punor reached for a pitchfork that was resting against the nearby wall.

The beast's gaze darkened, and he rose towards Punor.

Punor's heart began to race and his breath came quickly as he lunged towards the beast with the pitchfork.

The beast removed the pitchfork from his hand and said, "Give yourself a break and get some rest."

Punor moved away and didn't look back, but the muffled curse from the beast chased after him. If only he could locate the golden apples, his life would change dramatically and he would be wealthy and safe. In his perplexity he had no idea whose aid and advice he could trust.

As he walked through the streets, he heard his name mentioned. He was on guard; he had no intention of being attacked by anything. Monsters were everywhere he knew that.

Near the top of the hill he saw a little shepherd boy who was lying on the ground while a flock of sheep and lambs were grazing around him. He decided to rest nearby as darkness was now engulfing him. As he closed his eyes his mind began to play tricks on him, whereby he was responsible for a tribe of people who had survived a volcanic eruption.

A wolf howling at the full moon waked him. He rushed over to the shepherd boy to warn him that his flock was in danger. He patted him on the neck, "Wake up, there's a wolf roaming."

The shepherd boy's voice defied his size and stature, distinctive dark and rich of timbre as he bellowed his flock to move. At his age, the words sounded strange.

"Come on down with me and my flock, you've saved them. You should have some type of reward as is the custom around here."

"I don't know what or who to believe anymore. All I hear are lies, half-truths and secrets," Punor said as he followed the shepherd boy whose expression on his face was unreadable, although his eyes glittered feverishly.

"Have you a wife?" the shepherd boy asked.

"No," Punor replied.

"Well, as you saved my flock your reward will be my sister. You can marry her."

Punor bowed, his luck was changing. If they owned a flock, they had some money. Possibly even a house?

The sun began to rise as they entered a clearing where a small house stood. "This is your place as well now. Come meet my sister," he said.

Following him inside the house, Punor noted that although very small it felt cozy not crowded.

On sight of the sister, recognition passed over Punor's face immediately. If love alone was a measurement of success, the future of the three of them had a measure of hope.

He'd met her three years before. Gosh had so much happened to him in such a short period of time?

Her face hardly veiled her thoughts, and her expression was a simple one as the shepherd boy explained her fate and she busied herself in the tidy kitchen, washing the dishes.

Punor couldn't believe it! This was turning out much better than he could have even hoped. His mind was thrown into frenzy.

"This will not be an ill-sorted marriage. I fell in love with your sister, three years ago and then I lost her when the death dealer and Jove were battling for my soul."

He moved towards her and kissed her, "Thank goodness, I found you. Will you marry me?"

She smiled, "Yes! I thought I'd lost you forever."

And so they were married, and they all lived happily ever after."

Assignment Fifty Seven - Jannette was tired of being trapped in a place

4th September 2021

J.M. had a nightmare as not only did she get the character name incorrect, she also did not get the first line correct. As we use these homeworks as potential competition entries, attention to detail is a must. In terms of the story, J.M. used this as a vehicle to test a potential novel plot, which did not really lead into a positive short story experience.

Michael had great fun with another piece of fan fiction, which the group identified far quicker than he expected. S.J. complimented him on the blurb, something that we have been working to improve.

S.J. was very happy with this piece, and has entered it into a 2022 short story competition. The group agreed that it was very atmospheric and enthralling, touching on disturbing subjects without sensationalising them.

High Haven.

By

J.M. McKenzie

Jeanette lives in a small, isolated settlement that survived The Fall. She has heard stories about other communities full of new people and new opportunities and new ways of life. Her parents and the elders are secretive and full of foreboding about tales of such peoples and places, but Jeanette wants to find out for herself. She has to know.

Jeanette was tired of living in a place like High Haven. She yearned to be somewhere different. Somewhere bigger and better. Or maybe just somewhere different, with new people with new things to say. New things to see and do. New opportunities. Somewhere where life was fuller, less predictable, less certain. She had heard tales of a city. A lost city in the wetlands that had survived The Fall. A city of huge, tall buildings made of stone where hundreds of people lived and worked and prospered. She didn't know if it was real or just a legend, but she knew that she had to find out.

But, with three months to go until her 18th year, she knew she was running of time. On the day she turned 18 she was to be bonded with Jon from the Reader family. They had been promised to each other the day she was born. From then her life would be mapped out like that of her mother and her mother's mother before her. Work, eat, sleep and bear and raise children. Raise her children, her children's children and if she was lucky, her grandchildren's children after that.

The years stretched out before her like an endless monotonous path. Jeanette didn't want this. She wanted more.

Hers was the fourth generation of tree dwellers. Her great grandparents had come here when her grandparents were still small children to escape The Great Flood of 2025. They had built it with their own bare hands. Her great grandfather was a woodsman, a carpenter, like her grandfather and her father and now like her brother William. It was they who maintained the network of platforms, shelters, walkways, and ladders in which her family had lived for forty-seven years.

They were not alone. Her mother had told them at the time of The Fall, there were just six people living in just three roughly constructed platforms. Now, there were 36, 37 if you included the baby that Elspeth from the Cooper family had given birth to yesterday evening, living in a network of eleven self-contained, water-tight, predator-safe sleeping cabins in the highest part of the forest with communal washing, cooking, and eating areas lower down. Her father had divided their own cabin into three separate areas for him and her mother, her brother and her.

It was here that she now lay now in the dark on her small deerskin, feather-filled mattress, contemplating the day ahead with both fear and exhilaration. She would leave just before first light. Late enough to be safe from the predators that roamed the forest at night but early enough to be gone before her mother and father were awake. She was prepared. She had been sneaking small morsels of food up to her den every day for weeks now, dried meat, berries and seeds and shavings of mushrooms. Her food pouch was fat and tight, and she had filled her water pouch the night before. It was enough. Enough to enable her to keep moving for the first day when the likelihood of her being found and caught was highest. Later she would have time to forage for more.

Only the men were permitted to leave the settlement and then only once or twice a month in groups to hunt. Women and children stayed close to home to work and gather. Always close enough to scurry up the ladders when the alarm bell sounded that danger was near. The elders told horrible tales of woman and children that had strayed too far in the past and been taken by wolves and bears. Besides they said, there was nothing beyond the trees. Nothing except the barren wasteland at the edge of the forest and the desolate wetlands beyond.

But Jeanette knew differently. She had seen the strange and mysterious objects that some of the men brought back from their extended hunting trips. Seen the way the elders had examined them with frowns and murmured exclamations before secreting them away in their cabins away from the prying eyes of the children. She had felt the thrill of excited curiosity bubbling under the surface of the camp whenever anything was found. Seen the shine in her father's eyes and the flush on her mother's cheeks whenever something of particular significance was found.

She had asked her parents about it. Why the adults were so secretive about it. Her father had been angry, or maybe upset it was hard to tell, shouting about destabilising the community, about dangers she could never understand, about how her foolish snooping would be the death of her. But her mother had said that soon she would find out. Soon, when she was old enough, she would be told about the objects and where they came from. That she must be patient. She would understand everything in time.

But she didn't have time. Didn't want to be patient. She wanted to know everything now.

Then, a few weeks ago she had seen one of these objects. Her father had borrowed it from Eli Bains. He and her mother had been looking at it in their sleeping space. She heard them whispering and sighing over it one evening after supper before the fall of night. Then, the alarm had sounded, and they had hurried out to see what was wrong. Her father hurried down to the forest floor to help deal with a fox had strayed inside the fence and was after their chickens and his mother stood on the platform to watch.

She crept into their room and saw the object lying on their mattress. It was a narrow oblong of faded red with symbols engraved on its outer cover. She picked it up. The outer cover was firm and smooth under her fingers. She ran them over the engravings. Small lines and curves and dots and dashes that she didn't understand. The cover parted and the object opened upon three sides. Inside were hundreds of wafer-thin, parched, and yellowing leaves. They two were covered in row after row of tiny symbols like the ones on the cover but smaller and darker. The leaves fluttered between her fingers and one of them crumbled under her touch, flakes drifted into fur of the bedcover. She guiltily tried to brush them away and jumped up as she heard mother returning from outside.

She was still in the doorway when her mother entered the sleeping space. Jeanette turned to face her, and her mother's eyes shot immediately to the object on the bed. A flicker of alarm crossed her face. She looked at it and back at Jeanette, uncertainty creasing her brow.

"What is it, Mother?"

"You'll find out all in time, Jeanette."

"What is it, Mother? Please."

Her mother glanced outside towards the ladder. They could hear male voices shouting and chickens squawking beneath them.

"It's called a *book*," her mother whispered. "It's from before The Fall. Now, go to bed!"

A *book*. A BOOK! Jeanette had turned the word over and over in her mind. She'd heard of books but never seen one. When people had first come here, they had come with nothing. They had fled their homes in nothing but the clothes on their backs. Before she died, her great-grandmother had spoken to Jeanette and brother about books. She had told them they were full of knowledge and wonder and voices from long ago. She was even able remembered some of the stories in books she had seen before The Fall. Tales of princes and princesses and evil stepmothers and animals that could talk. Jeanette thought of the inanimate red object on the bed and wondered how it told its stories. She had always imagined it would speak the words it had to tell but now it dawned on her that they were be contained somehow, in the tiny rows of symbols on the leaves.

From that moment there was no doubt in her mind that she must leave. She had to know what lay beyond the forest. She had to find the place the book came from. She wanted to see more. To know more. To learn more.

As the sky began to change from black to grey, she tiptoed from her sleeping space and climbed carefully down the ladder. She moved quickly and quietly across the compound to the fence, her footsteps silenced by the cushion of fallen pine needles beneath her feet. She skirted past Frank Greaves who was on night watch to the broken section of the fence at the south-east corner where she had already dug out a crawl space and covered it with branches. She dragged away the branches and wriggled through. They'd know how she got out when they realsied she was gone but it didn't matter now. She would be long gone by then and she knew how to cover her tracks.

She let her eyes adjust to the darkness. An owl hooted and small creatures of the night rustled in the undergrowth. Somewhere on the mountain, a wolf howled, and she shivered but reminded herself that they would be heading back to their lairs before sunrise. They never hunted during the day. Using the shadow of the trees against the lightening sky as her guide to the path below, she began to run. She ran without looking back. She ran without stopping driven by the need to reach the stream that she knew ran south of the compound before it was light. She would enter the water and follow the stream south-west until she was out of the forest making it impossible for them to follow her tracks. Only then would she stop to rest.

The sun was high in the sky by the time the trees thinned out and stopped. She was tired and thirsty, and her feet were cold. It was a warm day and she set her moccasins on a rock to dry in the sun. Her toes were pale and wrinkled and she let the sun warm them too, wiggling them as she ate a strip of dried rabbit and a handful of seeds and dried berries. Her plan now was to head directly south towards the wetlands. She had never been outside the compound before, let alone the forest, and she should have been afraid, but she was not. She was nervous, of course. But also elated and buzzing with energy and anticipation. She had heard it said that the wetlands were a five day walk from High Haven, but she couldn't be sure. It could be more. It could be less. It wasn't the sort of information that anyone would willingly share with a girl. Why would a girl need to know something like that?

And indeed, it was for five days that she walked. She walked when it was light, stopping only to eat and drink, and slept when it was dark, finding a sheltered place to nestle down between a couple of rocks or bushes. She knew and hoped she was safe from predators in the wastelands, as they stuck to the forest where prey was plentiful and the wooded environment perfect for stealth and a surprise attack. But foraging was more of a challenge than she had anticipated. Vegetation of any kind was few and far between and when she did come across any shrubs or plants, she didn't recognise the small, wizened fruits and pods that grew on their sparse, woody branches. There was water. There was plenty of that in the streams and ponds that crisscrossed the landscape, but she struggled to find any that she could drink as most of it was as it was brown and gritty.

She kept herself going by constantly congratulating herself that she had finally done it. She almost couldn't believe it; she had dreamt about it for so many years. Couldn't believe she hadn't been followed, captured, and returned home to face the wrath of her parents and the elders. Sometimes, she even imagined she heard someone or something behind her. The snap of a twig underfoot or the crunch of gravel. She would spin around and scan the landscape back in the direction she had come, but there was nothing or no one to be seen. The grey green boglands stretched out it as far as she could see, bleak and still.

By the morning of the fifth day, she was weak and tired, and her feet were sore and blistered. Hungry and thirsty, her lips dry and cracked and her vision blurred, she was seriously considering turning back. She was beginning to think she had made a mistake. Doubting herself. Maybe everyone was right. Maybe there was nothing out here. Maye it was all gone. The feeling that she was being followed was stronger than ever. She recognised that it was a hallucination, brought on by anxiety, exhaustion and dehydration and she pushed the idea away.

It was getting harder and harder to walk. Head down, she forced herself to put one foot in front of the other and keep moving. She could barely see. Her head was pounding. She stumbled and fell to her knees tipping forward so that she was on all fours with her head hanging low. It was no good. She could go no further, and she didn't have the strength to go back. What had she done? It was over. It was all over. What a fool she had been. Why hadn't she listened to her parents. Why couldn't she had been happy with the life that she had.

She raised her head and crawled forward a few paces and then she saw it. Just like that! The land in front of her dropped away and down into a wide flat valley. The floor of the valley was covered with structures like nothing she had ever seen before. Hundreds of tall angular grey buildings, of different heights, shapes, and sizes. All crowded together like a clump of mushrooms on the forest floor. All dotted with row after row of tiny windows. The buildings were clustered around a vast river. Another huge grey structure spanned the river but this one was curved and elegant. The river flowed out to what she could only guess was the ocean. Her grandfather had once told her about the ocean. She had found it hard to imagine so much water. Impossible to visualise and yet now she was looking it for real. She rubbed her eyes with her filthy fingers and wiped away the tears that trickled down her cheeks. She had made it. She had found the lost city. It was real and it was beautiful.

She stumbled down the valley.

As she got closer, details she hadn't seen from above gradually began to appear. The ground between the buildings was overgrown with greenery, deep fissures in the earth sprouting all manner of course weeds and shrubs. The buildings themselves were tainted green by the moss and creepers that blanketed their walls. It was as the city itself was one with nature. But not in a good way. Vermin scurried in and out of in piles of rubble and rusting piles of metal. Plumes of dark smoke spiraled from windows and rooftops. Rickety looking wooden structures cross-crossed between the buildings. And there was a smell. A bad smell. A smell of mould and decay. Up close the city wasn't beautiful at all. It was ugly. And where were all the people?

As if to answer her question, she heard a whistle, and something rushed past her ear and thudded into a doorframe beside her. She looked at it, quivering in the crumbling wood. An arrow! Suddenly, she was afraid.

She ducked inside the doorway and huddled down in the corner of the room inside. It was dark and wet and smelt of must and rotting leaves. She heard scuttling footsteps and whispered voices. They seemed to be all around her. Her heart pounded in her chest. He breath caught in her throat.

And then she heard a series of grunts and thumps and yelps of pain. The scuttling footsteps receded and disappeared, and a large dark figure appeared in the doorway, silhouetted against the light outside. He rushed across to her and put one hand on the back of her head and the other over her mouth. She struggled and fought to escape his grip. He spoke in a harsh whisper.

"Jeanette, it's me! Don't be afraid. Be quiet. They have gone. For Now. But we must get away."

"Father!" She burrowed her face into his chest. "Father, I'm so sorry. I'm so sorry. I wanted ... I thought ..."

"I know. I know. We can talk about that later. Now, I have come to take you home."

A Day of Destiny

by

Michael Andrews

Newtons Third Law states that for every action there is an opposite and equal reaction. In this example, one man's salvation is another woman's doom...

Jannette was tired of being trapped in a place from where she knew that she could not escape. Each morning, she went through the same routine; the harsh shrill of the alarm, pulling her from the land of Nod, the pain in her hand as she thumped the top of said alarm, grimacing in a pained but satisfied feeling of momentary power as the offending clock smashed into a dozen pieces.

This morning was no different, but did she really expect it to be? Hope was futile, she had learned that now. Rubbing her hand, Jannette pulled back the duvet, shivering as the cold chill of the winter air wafted across the room from the ill-fitting window of the apartment that she had rented for the occasion.

Pulling on her dark blue bathrobe, she skipped across the icy floor into the bathroom, hoping against hope that this time, the shower would reward her with hot water but as she turned the faucet, her body was already shivering in anticipation of the cold waterfall of droplets that dripped their way onto her thin body. Resigning herself to yet another cold shower, Jannette quickly lathered her shower gel over her body and washed it clean, grabbing the towel to dry herself before re-robing in her dressing gown in a half-hearted attempt to warm up.

Sitting on her bed, she pulled out the newspaper cutting that she had kept. It seemed to be the only piece of evidence that she was not going crazy but who else would believe her story. 3rd February 1993. Tomorrow's date.

Maybe I'll get him today, she mused as she stared at the face of the smiling man. She felt a sense of longing in her body, the way that his eyes seemed to have an eternal youth, a playful and mischievous twinkle in his deep brown eyes. His mouth had a boyish smile as though he had achieved everything that he wanted from life.

"Fuck you!" Jannette snarled and ripped up the cutting into small pieces, scattering them across the floor as she aimed futilely at the small bin.

She flicked on the radio to break the silence, only to swear at herself as she had forgotten to change the station. The opening lines of Sonny and Cher's most famous song filled the room.

"I got you Babe," Jannette hissed. "I'll fucking get you this time, you rat bastard."

Stomping across the bedroom to the wardrobe, she flung the doors open and looked inside. Five different outfits hung, waiting for her to choose. As with every morning, she tried to push her hand towards the elegant lilac dress, but her hand had a mind of its own.

Sighing to herself, she dressed in the smart black trouser suit that she always wore when going on camera.

Grabbing her coat, she opened the door and went out onto the street.

Snow had fallen, it always did on the 2nd of February. At least, each 2nd of February this year. Pulling on her coat, she stepped off the pavement and straight into a puddle of icy cold water.

"Every bloody time!" she cursed.

"Watch out for that first step, it's a doozy!" a man called out with a chuckle in his voice.

"Fuck off Ned!" Jannette flipped the obnoxious insurance salesman the finger and shook her foot. She clutched her bag under her arm and headed towards the park.

Gobbler's Knob was packed, as it was every same day; the citizens of Punxsutawney, Pennsylvania waiting with eager anticipation for the emergence of the vermin that was the only reason this shithole of a town was on the map at all.

"Jannette, there you are," Jack Halbrook said, handing her a paper cup of coffee. "We are fighting for space today, especially with Phil Connors being in town."

"Do you think we can get close to him?"

"I thought you hated him?"

"I do... but there's no harm in getting ourselves near the crowd, is there?"

"I guess..."

"Who's the star here?" Jannette snapped and stomped off towards the bandstand where the *important* dignitaries of the town had gathered.

"Not you, for sure," Jack muttered under his breath, but picked up his camera and followed her.

A large crowd had gathered around a man in a dark woollen coat. Jack instantly recognised him, everyone did. He had become a well-loved celebrity in the town almost overnight, a massive change from the obnoxious, stuck-up presenter that Jack had met the year before.

Jack noticed Jannette rummaging around in her bag. He was about to tell her that he still had her microphone when his eyes widened.

"It's all your fucking fault, Connors!" Jannette yelled, brandishing a small handgun in the air. "I was supposed to be the star, not you! You've trapped me here and this is the only way out!

"GUN!" Someone shouted and people turned in Jannette's direction. A policeman pulled out his sidearm and yelled a warning.

Jannette's eyes were fixed firmly on the man holding the microphone who still seemed oblivious to her approach. She felt a dull ache in her left shoulder before more pain erupted in her chest. She fell backwards to the ground, gazing down in disbelief at the growing patches of crimson that were ruining her best pristine white blouse. A smile spread across her mouth.

"Please let this time be the end," she whispered as Jack reached her side, frantically pressing down on the many bullet wounds. Her vision faded into black as she heard Phil's voice begin.

"Welcome one and all to Punxsutawney, Pennsylvania, where the crowds are gathered in anticipation."

The harsh shrill of the alarm pulled Jannette from the land of Nod. Her hand felt the pain of the smashed clock as she pulled back the duvet. Switching on the radio, she sighed as she heard the fateful words once again over the top of the intro to the most famous song by Sonny and Cher.

"Okay campers, rise and shine. Don't forget your booties today cos it's cold outside... it's GROUNDHOG DAY!!"

Taken
By
S.J.Gibbs

Jannette Bird had disappeared one late afternoon on her way home from school. Would she ever be reunited with her family again?

Jannette was tired of being trapped in a place. Although she could walk and run, she was in no position to do so, as her circumstances were more than awkward. Her face blazed red from exertion, her eyes glowed brightly and yet she'd not moved from the sofa, all morning. The room smelled familiar, safe.

Of course deep down she knew this not to be true and so did he.

She heard his voice. She dug her fingers into the sofa.

It was a visit she'd been expecting, but hoping not to get.

His voice was controlled, being in control was important to him. When he spoke it was as though he was reading from a script, the words always in the same format.

Her stomach began to feel uneasy, as he moved towards her and untied her.

With ruthless disregard and for most dramatic effect he slowly undressed her and moved is fingers slowly over her now naked body. There was no point trying to assert herself, it only caused more pain. The act of what he was about to do was inevitable.

She turned her head towards the hallway to try and block the sight of his face, and tried to swallow the lump that insisted on staying in her throat as she bit back the tears.

Although he was fast to reach his climax, to her it seemed deadly slow.

The room was muggy and dark, curtains drawn, almost eerie as she watched him tie her hands and feet once more before he left and locked the door.

She lay motionless, unable to do or think anything right now, as she observed the sun just appearing from behind the heavy curtains. Sleep overcame her, and distant voices spoke in her head.

A sound broke her stillness. A car, a different engine, she didn't need proof of that; she knew the sound of his.

How long had it been since she'd heard anything from outside the room other than him?

She released the breath she held. Could this be her way out? Her cheeks flushed hot with blood. Was this her chance?

She peered towards the curtains. Everything was silent the car engine had stopped. She could hear a pin drop, the silence was so deafening.

It must be a dream, she thought sluggishly but she reached out her hands to look at the bindings. She could call out, scream but he was still in the house and if nobody heard her he'd beat her like he had before and tape her mouth once more like he'd done when she'd first been here.

Footsteps! He was coming down the stairs. She looked around the small, plain room, which had been her prison for so long. The year she'd been taken was 2015, she knew that but what year was it now? She'd been just 15 years old.

Entertainment was all she was to him.

More footsteps! This time outside, the crunch of gravel. She needed to be clever.

Her natural desire was to scream for help. A profound sadness enveloped her, in case she should lose this opportunity.

Determination drove her forward as she hopped towards the curtains, her frown fierce with concentration not to trip.

Eagerly she reached them, and using her head she began to try and open a gap, assisted by her hands, which were bound together, scared to death he would enter the room and discover what she was attempting to do. She knew outside was open ground and flat with nothing around for miles.

The front door opened, she could hear his voice and now the voice of another male, a Jehovah's Witness trying to talk to him about God!

A gap had opened she could see him now. She raised her bound hands above her head and placed them in a prayer position, and pushed her face towards the windowpane. All she needed now was for him t glance her way, when she would mouth 'HELP'!

She studied him, her potential saviour; he was smart wearing a dark suit. She began to whisper inaudibly over and over, 'HELP' almost crying at the thought that he may not look in the direction of the window.

The conversation broke; he was closing the front door. She began to shiver as the man of God, began to retrace his steps across the gravel towards his car. She started to sob bitterly; he wasn't going to see her.

Her energy began to fade.

He was in front of his car now, and she willed him to turn around and spot her.

Suddenly as he opened the driver's door to the car, she saw him glance her way. She tasted the bitterness of reality as she mouthed 'HELP'. Had he seen her? She couldn't be sure.

As he drove away, she dropped to the floor.

Would she ever be found? Did her family even believe she was still alive? Was anyone even still looking for her? Her attention shifted to him, as she ran the fingers of her bounded hands over the two small scars on her neck, terrified that if he knew she'd attempted to cry for help he may cut her again.

Music started to play, which was a good sign, as it tended to occupy him for a while. She stood and closed the gap in the curtains the best she could and hopped back to the sofa.

How many summers and winters had she lived here for, how many years? Although unsure she thought this to be her sixth summer.

It was comforting to think that the man of God had glanced her way, but it didn't resolve her concerns. What if he hadn't seen her plea for help?

Food was scarce, some days he didn't feed her at all and today he'd offered her nothing as yet. She drove the desire of hunger from her mind, as she'd learned to do. She focused instead on holidays by the sea, which she'd happily spent with her parents and her little sister, Indiana.

The music stopped, she could hear him pacing.

Too tired to fight her tears anymore, she let them fall and sat shaking, glancing around the small empty room.

Who was she trying to deceive? The man of God had not seen her, she was almost sure.

Rivulets of sweat ran down her body. The pacing stopped. She hoped he'd fallen asleep.

She began to cough, her chest was getting worse. Sometimes she could barely breathe. She breathed in trying to remember the smell of the sea.

As the memory flooded back into her nostrils she said aloud, "It's wonderful."

The key turned in the door. He hadn't fallen asleep. He had other plans.

"Good girl for staying quiet when our unexpected visitor came," he said without heat.

Although she knew it was pointless, she still pleaded, "Please let me go. Let me out!"

"That's enough. You know that can't happen, " his dark brows crouched over hiss equally dark eyes.

"Why are you always so positively rude? Why can't you just be happy here with me?" he continued.

"Because I'm your prisoner and I don't want to be here. I want to go home to my family," she said dryly.

He looked gravely at her tousled hair, as he approached her, "You're beginning to smell again, time for a shower."

The word 'shower' revived images that earlier experiences had engraved on her brain, "Please no! I don't smell I'm fine."

He untied her hands and feet and dragged her across to the door, which she leant against before venturing forward.

She was in no mood for a catfight with him o she surrendered to his will and moved towards the stairs, knowing she'd be no match for him anyway.

He tugged at her hair, "C'mon, hurry up! Stop dawdling."

She knew if she struggled, he would apply added force from his rugged repertoire.

Once under the shower, the further humiliation took its normal course, as he ordered her to strike poses as he snapped still shots from his camera.

What could she do other than to obey his orders? She glanced away and then back at him, trying not to take in the sickly expression on his face, the stress of the situation was becoming too much for her. She was scared, but she'd pulled through this many times before. He made her feel as though she was nothing more than some type of wild animal.

Placing his camera down, he moved towards her, stripped off his own clothes and entered the shower, wrapping his arms around her. This was always the worst part when he began to cry the soul-deep sobs as if he was remembering something awful from his own youth.

A male voice's stunned tone drew her attention beyond the shower to the doorway, "Move away from her now if you know what's good for you."

The police officer seized the moment and dragged him from the shower. "Jannette Bird, is that really you? Have we really found you after all these years?"

Another officer wrapped a towel around her as Jannette cried, "I want my mother. I want to see my mother."

She watched as they handcuffed him roughly and the officer who'd handed her the towel said, "You poor kid. Thank God we've found you. An anonymous call was put in that somebody was being held here under suspicious circumstances. Six years you've been missing, but we never gave up hope that one day we'd find you."

She blinked her eyes, barely able to believe what was happening as they radioed it in to the station and requested a back up car and for female officers to attend. He was led away and placed into the back of the police car.

Her tears flowed.

Less than an hour later, she was sat in the police station waiting for her mother, father and Indiana to arrive. The end of the ordeal was over with and the start of her old life was beginning, now at the age of twenty-one. Six years had been cruelly stolen from her, she would never be the innocent fifteen year old again who was taken as she ambled home from school, one late afternoon.

JAMS Publishing

Assignment Fifty Eight - A cuddle with Libbie might help to relieve some tension

1st October 2021

Yet another S.J. prompt which we all balked at but ended up with varied pieces.

J.M. went back to her zombie roots with a tale of surviving the apocalypse. It received mixed comments from the group, resulting from it being partly a monologue as well as reminding the group about a certain scene from The Walking Dead.

Michael struggled with this piece, writing it at the last moment and as such, while the premise was good, it lacked the depth and description needed to carry it off.

S.J. wrote a very short piece, which came over as a little rushed, with another weak ending, and her predilection for deaths!

Libbie's Kiss.

By

J.M. McKenzie

Israel has a had a tough day. A cuddle and maybe even a kiss from Libbie might make things better. It's not going to be easy though ...

A cuddle with Libbie might help to relieve some tension right now, Israel thought as he hammered the last of the nails into the floorboards he had pulled up to use as a barricade for the front door. He'd had a terrible day. He was utterly stressed out and exhausted He felt so alone. So hopeless. So terribly, terribly sad. Yes, a cuddle, and maybe even a kiss, was exactly what he needed.

And just like that, his mind was made up. It had been too long. *Way* too long. He'd have to work up to it of course. It wasn't going to be easy. She wasn't going to be ... *keen*. Not after ... everything. But she'd come around. If he was careful, sensitive, approached her gently. Yes! It was decided. He was going to do it. But later. When he was ready. After dinner.

Even by the standard of the continuous stream of tough days that had gone on since the start of the outbreak, it had been a particularly tough day. Their water had run out. Well, not exactly run out, rather the last remaining container in the cupboard under the stairs had turned out to be undrinkable. It was an old jerry can that they had fished out of the garage back at the start when they were filling everything they could lay their hands on with water from the taps before they ran dry.

He was sure they'd rinsed it out properly at the time. He was usually so meticulous about stuff like that that. But when he opened it, the acrid reek of petrol burned the back of his throat and a rainbow-coloured film swirled on the surface of the water. He considered drinking it anyway. Hang the consequences. But that would have been downright stupid. The last thing he needed now was to poison himself. That wasn't going to help his situation in the slightest. He had no idea what consuming petrol would do to him, but he was sure it wouldn't be good. It would almost certainly be painful and unpleasant. No! Drinking contaminated water was not an option.

Then he got angry with himself for being so careless. It was so unlike him. He was so meticulous about stuff like that. How could he have been so irresponsible. What had he been thinking? Had he even been thinking? But who knew what sort of state he'd been in back then? They'd been in. They had been crazy days. He'd been out of his mind most of the time. They both had. It was amazing that he'd even had the presence of mind to think about storing water. It was all they could do just to stay alive. Just to get through each day without dying. So what if they'd made one mistake. It wasn't surprising. It wasn't the end of the world.

But then a little voice in the back of his head began to niggle at him. Telling him another story. He tried to push it away, but it kept coming back. Chattering. Whispering. It wasn't him. It couldn't have been. He knew *he* wouldn't have filled a dirty container with water that they intended to drink. There was no way, even if he wasn't in his right mind, that he would have done something like that. He just wouldn't. It wasn't how he operated. No. It had to have been Libbie. That was the only logical explanation. Dreamy, ditsy beautiful Libbie. It was exactly the sort of thing she would do. They had both been filling up containers that day. She never paid attention to detail like that. Her head had always been in the clouds. Even before.

And just like that he was angry. No, not angry, furious. He was furious!

Libbie! Libbie! How could you have been so careless. So stupid. What were you thinking? That was your problem! You never thought! Never paid attention! Never listened. You were always dreaming. Always off somewhere in your head. Oh Libbie! Oh Libbie. WHY WERE YOU SUCH A FOOL?

He punched the wall until his hand bled. His entire body shook with rage. Tears of frustration poured down his cheeks. He grabbed a cushion from the sofa and screamed into it silently. He fell to his knees, and he wept.

Later, when he'd pulled himself together, he set about leaving the house to get more water. It was time to stop thinking about who had done it or had not. About who was innocent or guilty. About who was to blame or who wasn't. It didn't matter. It was emotionally exhausting. Pointless. Draining. At the end of the day, it didn't even matter. Nothing did. It was simple. He needed water and he was just going to have to go out and get some. He was always going to have had to do this at some point. It was just that the moment had come sooner than expected.

And so, he had. He'd taken down the boards from the front door. He'd dressed in the heaviest clothing he could find. He made sure every inch of his body was covered.

Canvas work trousers and a parka jacket. Thick leather gloves. Heavy boots. A balaclava and ski goggles. It was September. It wasn't warm but it wasn't yet cold. He was sweating before he even left the house, but part of him knew it wasn't the clothes that were making him sweat. It was the fear. The fear of going outside.

He'd taken two empty containers and headed head straight for the river. Keeping low. Quiet. Scurrying from building to building. From bush to bush. He saw a few infected stumbling aimlessly around but kept well out of their way. He saw no other living. The other houses on his street were either derelict, with doors wide open and windows smashed or boarded up like theirs. Cars abandoned on driveways, doors ajar, boots open half-filled, the detritus of thwarted escape plans scattered on the ground. Odd shoes, backpacks, tattered clothing, kids' toys.

It only took him an hour to reach the river, fill the containers and return. Only an hour but for every minute of that hour, every second, he was filled with dread. Expectation at every moment to turn a corner and come face to face with an infected. To come face to face with death... or worse.

When he finally closed the front door behind him, he sank to his knees, weeping with relief. His hands were still shaking when he started to pick up the boards and hammer them back in place. He felt weak and wobbly, and his knees trembled. He had only managed to carry enough water for a week or so. The reality dawned on him that he was going to have to do this again. And then again after that. Again, and again and again. His food supplies were running low too. How long could he go on like this. What was the point? What was the point of anything anymore?

That night, for dinner he drank the can of condensed milk that he'd been saving for a special occasion. For a day when he really needed a boost. When he needed the comfort that only something sweet and creamy could provide. Creamy decadence of thick sweetened milk. He opened a lip of the can and bent back the thin metal before pouring the contents into his mouth in a steady rippling trickle. It was everything he had imagined it would be. Thick, sweet, and decadent. It dribbled down his chin into his beard. He wiped it away and licked his fingers. Libbie would be horrified. What she didn't know wouldn't hurt her.

He looked around the room. At the boarded-up windows. The boarded-up door. At the greasy pillows and dirty blankets on the sofa where he had slept fitfully and alone every night for more nights than he could care to remember. At the empty cans and food packaging scattered on the floor. At the remnants of last night's fire in the hearth. He'd burned through most of their furniture. Everything that would burn that was or would burn without choking him to death on noxious fumes. All the books were gone, and the dining table and chairs. He was half way through dismantling the book case now. It didn't look like their home any more. It looked like a vagrant's shelter. It smelt like one too. It smelt of sweat and smoke and piss.

It was time to go and see Libbie. Time for that cuddle.

Libbie was hunched in the shadows in the far corner of the room. Her head snapped up when Israel entered, and her bloodshot eyes locked with his. The chains around her wrists rattled then pulled taught as she lurched for him. Green spittle drooled from her snarling and hissing mouth.

Israel took a step towards her.

"It's all right my darling. I'm not going to hurt you," he whispered. "I just want to ... hold you. I want you to ... hold me."

Another step. She quietened. For a moment he thought he saw a flicker of recognition in her eyes. Thought she understood. She froze with her arms outstretched. Her mouth hung open.

Israel sighed and stepped into her embrace.

Libbie's Introduction to Jasper

by

Michael Andrews

When Jasper is introduced to Libbie, it looks like love at first sight. But is it all that it seems?

A cuddle from Libbie might help to relieve some tension. That is what Maddie thought. She watched as her five-year-old daughter nervously tiptoed into the lounge, expectant eyes on her.

Libbie bit her lip, her dark brown eyes were wide as she studied the people in the room. Her parents were there, of course, as were her Aunt Bree and Uncle Kenny. She tugged at her flowery nightdress as she walked into the middle of the room.

"Come here, Libbie, my darling," Maddie smiled sweetly at her daughter. Flashing a look across at the gathered crowd of family and friends, she wondered not for the first time if they were doing the correct thing. "Come give Jasper a cuddle."

Jasper walked slowly across the room towards the young girl. He could smell the fear on her. His own body was shaking with tension, but as his own dark brown eyes met the five-year old's, Jasper knew that he was in love already.

Jasper felt the hair on the back of his neck prickle as the young girl wrapped her bare arms around his neck. A low rumble in the back of his throat made the girl shiver but he rubbed his face against hers to calm her down.

Libbie giggled as she felt the soft hair caress her smooth cheek.

"That's it," Freddie smiled, as he watched his daughter smile break across her face. He knew that this would be good for her. That Jasper was exactly what she needed, and also that Libbie would be perfect for Jasper. He had been through so much in his 56 years. So much pain, so much loneliness but Freddie knew that his daughter would solve that.

"Mummy," Libbie whispered as she rubbed her hands through the hair on Jasper's back. "I love him already!"

"I knew you would, my darling," Maddie smiled. "And look, Jasper's tail is showing how much he loves you as well."

Libbie giggled as she watched the Labrador's tail wagging back and forth.

"Ew!" Libbie wiped her cheek as Jasper's long wet tongue licked her face.

"Now Libbie," Freddie said, stroking both his daughter's and their new dog's head. "Jasper is a rescue dog and has been hurt, so we need to give him lots of love."

"Oh Daddy," Libbie gushed as she hugged Jasper tighter. "I will never hurt Jasper. I love him so much already."

That night, Maddie and Freddie opened the door to their daughter's bedroom. As much as they had promised themselves that they would not let the dog sleep upstairs, they simply could not separate the pair.

Jasper glanced across as the faint light from the landing flickered across the bedroom. His chest rose up and down, breathing easy as he realised that this time, he was in a safe, loving home.

The Vaccine
By
S.J.Gibbs

Would a vaccine for the deadly virus ever be found?

A cuddle with Libbie might help to relieve some tension. The rest of the night was Den's to spend as he pleased.

He held her tight, but how could he remain calm in times like these? He glanced at his watch, and sighed.

The long hours of hard work had taken their toll on him. He was so tired and yet he found it so difficult to rest his mind or his body.

Moving from the bed where Libbie lay, he stood and stared out of the window.

Libbie's voice cracked with nervousness, "Are you okay? Are you coming back to bed?"

Harassed he snapped back at her, "I can't sleep. I'm heading downstairs."

"So I get to spend another night on my own?"

Den was tired of fighting, tired of her attitude towards his work, tired of everything.

Tears were already rising in her eyes. He walked out of the bedroom, unable to face her anymore. He was losing is mind, living a nightmare.

Once downstairs in the kitchen, he took a juicy pear from the fruit bowl and munched on it.

Their home was lovely, spacious and nicely decorated but none of it held any meaning for him any longer.

For the last three months he'd barely left the lab, knowing he was so close to producing the vaccine, which could help to save humanity from the terrible virus, which was circulating and killing millions throughout the world.

Breathing hard, he knew that he needed sleep, but how could he when he was so near and could save so many lives. The reward of doing so outstretched the financial gains he would make, in his mind.

Suddenly he felt like a schoolboy on holiday as the final cog to the jigsaw twigged in his brain. He had the answer, the solution, he was so sure. The last piece of technology he needed to apply. He could achieve it; he needed to return to the lab immediately.

A few minutes later he reversed his car from the driveway, the lab and the vaccine calling him, although officially off duty for the night.

The speedometer registered 30 miles over the limit for the road and still he accelerated harder.

His new knowledge was of priceless value to the vaccine, of that he was confident. The thought soothed his head and the aches of his body.

Such sorrow had filled the world since the virus had first struck, over eighteen months ago, and now he was going to be able to change all of this with the world's first vaccine, something everyone had believed impossible.

A silly grin stretched across Den's face, and he didn't notice the car coming towards him on the wrong side of the road, it's dark form absent of headlights.

He was suddenly so far away, like in a dream, only this wasn't a dream as he stared down at his own crumpled dead body in the carnage of the two mangled vehicles.

Everything around him was so quiet.

His spirit kneeled down beside the car, memories flashed before him.

Mortification struck him at the reality of his situation. His body was dead, but his soul was still alive. He would no longer be able to carry out his good works of the vaccine. His knowledge could no longer be used by humanity, it had died along with his body.

Assignment Fifty Nine – You wake up all alone

29th October 2021

J.M. wrote a very atmospheric, post-apocalyptic story, which was not as predictable as the group thought. A clever twist left the group wanting more.

Michael split opinion once again. He wanted to get into the mind of an evil murderer, to help him along in his current work in progress, and the group found the story very disturbing, horrifying and graphic. As such, the readers, *especially Michael's mother*, are once again warned about upsetting scenes. In the words of Earnest Hemmingway, "write drunk edit sober", as Michael did admit to having written this after a night out.

S.J. was very happy with this piece, even though she wrote this in the first person present tense. The group feel that some of her best work is written in this style. Again, she has entered this into a competition where she eagerly awaits the results.

Gone.

By

J.M. McKenzie

Deb knows something is wrong the moment she wakes up. Its too quiet, too bright and her husband is missing.

I know something isn't right as soon as I awake. The sense of a cold empty space beside me in the bed. The silence. The stillness. The emptiness of the air. I drift between sleep and wakefulness for a few moments then I open my eyes. Something about the quality of the light is wrong. It's late.

A close my eyes again and try to remember what day it is. It must be Sunday. But no, yesterday was Tuesday! I went to work. We both did. I was in the office by seven, to grab some uninterrupted time to work on a big project proposal before my back-to-back client meetings from nine till five. After writing up the outcomes of the day's meetings, I left the office at seven, as usual.

Chris, who always gets home around six (he's not as sold on the concept of the 80-hour working week as I am), had cooked dinner by the time I got in and we ate around eight then watched a couple of episodes of Bridgerton before bed. No, it's not Sunday! It's Wednesday! *Shit*! I've slept through my alarm!

I sit bolt upright, now wide awake and panicking. Racking my brains to remember what I have in my diary this morning. I reach for my phone. It's on charge and I yank it from the thin white cable to look at the screen. It's black. I tap it a few times and then press the power button and hold it down. Nothing happens. *Shit*! It's dead. I roll over the bed onto my belly to look at the digital alarm clock on Chris's bedside table. Thank God he's such a technophobe. But Its screen is black too. A power cut. That must be it. The power must be off.

I sit up and listen for a tick or a creak from the bathroom radiator, or the soft rumble of the hot water tank in the loft. Nothing. Everything is off. That's it, That's definitely it. The power has gone off and so the boiler is off too. Damn it. Now, not only am I late, but there's no hot water either.

But where is Chris? Why didn't he wake me?

I get out of bed and go downstairs. The kitchen is cold and quiet and empty. The fridges are off. None of the clocks are working. The room feels like an echo chamber. The thermal blinds across the bifold doors at the back of the house are all down. They're electric. I pick up the remote control. It's dead too.

I go to the front window, where the blind is manual. I pull the cord to open it. The street outside is deserted. I'm confused. I'm beginning to feel anxious. Afraid, but I'm not sure why or what of. I press my face against the glass and crane to see up and down the street. No rushing traffic. No squealing children on their way to school. No scurrying dog walkers. No self-satisfied joggers.

I go to the front door and open it. I look up and down the street again. No-one. Nothing. Complete silence. Not even the tweet of a bird or the rustle of a leaf. Everything feels strange. Like the vacuum that is left in a sports stadium after all the fans have left. I slam the door closed and lean against it. I'm breathing fast and hard. My heart is pounding in my chest. I need to calm down. To think. There must be perfectly rational explanation for all of this. I'm being ridiculous.

I go back upstairs. I look out of the window in the spare room. Our car is parked outside our garage. So are those of all our neighbours. I need to get dressed and go outside. Find someone to talk to. To explain what is going on. I pull on a t-shirt and some leggings. As I shove my feet into my trainers, I run over the previous evening in my mind to see if there is anything that I have missed, or forgotten about today.

After Bridgerton, we went to bed. Chris had the TV on in the bedroom. He called through to me when I was brushing my teeth. I wasn't really listening. I was thinking about my project proposal.

"Hey, listen to this, Deb! A massive solar flare is on its way. It's gonna hit earth sometime during the night."

"Oh," I said through a mouthful of toothpaste. "And what does that mean?"

"Probably nothing. Maybe some power outages? IT problems? *Maybe*, it'll knock the earth off its axis, and we'll all wake up upside down!"

"Huh?"

"Just kidding. Mmm, you smell good. Come over here and *I'll* knock the earth off its axis for you!"

"You'll have to be quick! I've got an early start in the morning."

"When haven't you got an early start?"

"Sundays? I always have a lie in on Sundays. You know that ..."

"Oh, shut up and stop wasting good shagging time! Get over here!"

I giggled and jumped into bed, snuggling up against his warm body.

And what with *one thing and another* after that, I never gave the solar flare another thought.

A solar flare. Power outages. That must be it.

I go to the bathroom and wash my face. I look at myself in the mirror. A pair of anxious blue eyes with the remnants of yesterday's mascara still on the lashes, stare back at me. I run my fingers through my short dark hair, pushing it back from my face. I touch the long, curved scar on my forehead just below the hairline. I can feel the metal plate beneath it. The metal plate that they used to replace the piece of skull they took out to remove my brain tumour. The metal plate that saved my life seventeen years ago.

I go back downstairs and go outside. This time, with some relief, I see a figure shuffling up the street on the other side of the road. A man I think, but I can't tell who it is. He's too far away. I watch and wait as he approaches. I'm excited and nervous at the same time. Jittery. Maybe he'll know what's going on? He sees me. Crosses the street. He's coming towards me. As he gets closer, I notice his strange gait. He drags his left leg; his left arm hangs limply by his side and his head is at a funny angle on his neck.

Then I know who it is, and instantly my breath catches in my throat. My brain is rapidly trying to process something, but my mind is blocking it. *No!* It's trying to put together random pieces of information to give them meaning, but I can't allow it to take me there. It's too crazy. Too terrifying. Too plausible.

Joe Branston reaches my house. He stops at the gate and stares at me. He's not been right since the car accident three years ago that left him brain damaged. Disabled. The one thing I don't want to remember about Joe, pushes its way to the surface. I can't stop it. It freezes my blood in my veins. It makes the skin on my forearms tingle. It makes the hair on the back of my neck bristle. I feel sick. I look at Joe. I look at the white scar and the bald patch on the side of his head. I rub my own forehead again.

Joe Branston has a metal plate in his skull too.

My brain finally joins all the dots, makes the connections. I open my mouth and scream.

All alone for now

by

Michael Andrews

Henry has lost the love of his life. Can he replace her, or is he destined to be alone forever?

Blar blar blar blar

Reluctantly I open my eyes as the shrill of my alarm went off. Sighing, I wipe the sleep crusts from my eyelids. I look around the bedroom. The morning sunlight is seeping through the small slats of the beige blinds that are supposed to keep it out. *She* had drawn them, but the rays seep through anyway.

I roll over in my bed, pulling the duvet over me, wrapping myself in its warmth, trying to remember how her warmth felt like on my body. My face pressed into the pillow. The smell of her was still there. I breathed in deeply. I relaxed. It was almost as though she was still with me.

But she wasn't.

She isn't.

The smash of the lamp was what I needed to break me out of my daydream.

My hand slipped down to my crotch and I scratched the irritating problem around my lower regions. I sighed softly as I felt myself harden.

"Oh fuck yeah," I groaned. "Stroke it baby."

I imagined my hand was hers as I started to pump myself, bringing myself to a climax. My toes curled, my buttocks lifted off the bed as I felt the rush of my orgasm race through my body.

"FUCK YEAH!" I screamed, before collapsing back down, sweat pooling into my belly button as the high of the climax left my body.

Reaching over, I felt the damp towel on the bedside table and pulled back the duvet. Wiping myself down, the shivers started through my body. I saw the lines of white powder on the side and picked up the straw.

"FUUUUCK!" I gasped as the rush of the cocaine hit my brain. Twice more, I snorted the lines of fulfilment before stumbling towards the bathroom.

The toilet lid was down. I bumped across the walls as I tried to lift it before holding onto the sink basin.

"Ahhhhh!" The dark yellow stream whirlpooled down the plug hole.

That doesn't look right, I thought to myself but shrugged. Who gave a shit anyway? No-one cared about me. No-one cared about her. Why should I give a fuck about anything?

I didn't even bother to rinse the basin out. Why should I? Who cares about me anyway?

I stared into the mirror. A haunted look stared back. My once beautiful golden curly locks were now a matted, greasy mop of knotted filth. My once clean-shaven chin was covered with a food encased beard that curled at my nose and my chin. The red wine slobber from previous drinking was stained across the pieces of noodles and rice that threatened to finally escape their prison.

I sniffed at my armpit. Six months ago, I would have blanched at the stench, but no longer. Why did I need to? What did I have to live for? The smell was part of the new me. The better me. The strong me.

The me that would have given up. The me that would let myself give in to the desire in my body, my brain to end it all.

But that wasn't me anymore.

I ran the flannel under the warm tap, wiping the sweat from my armpits, cleaning off the drying semen from my crotch, feeling myself stir slightly as the warm cloth touched the hole inside my buttocks.

Staring once again into the mirror, I saw the darkness that shadowed my eyes, my soul and I knew that I needed to do something, anything, to stop the pain from hurting me once more.

The razor blades were there, on the side, beckoning to me. They laughed at me. I knew that they were my enemy, but they were my friends as well. They could give me that release. That moment of glorious sunshine as they cut into my skin, releasing the pain that had been building up inside of me.

Wetness dripped onto my toes. I glanced down to see the redness covering my little pinky tootsies. I had hated that word from my Granny but it had always stuck with me.

"Fuck this!" I yelled as I looked at the dripping blade in my hand, the cut on my wrist leaking blood. "You ... will ... not ... win!"

I grabbed a towel to stem the flow, which wasn't that deep and within minutes, it had stopped. Striding into the bedroom, I grabbed a shirt and a pair of loose-fitting joggers.

Running down the stairs, I could still smell her. Her stench was driving me crazy. I needed to get rid of it. I had to.

I threw open the cupboard door and there she was, in all of her glory.

Her smile was so large, it stretched from ear to ear, literally.

How could she not have loved me?

What did she think was wrong with me?

That fucking bitch!

That stupid, selfish cow!

I showed her! I knew that I would have been perfect for her but no. ... she said no!

She *had a husband and daughter already...* the fucking, lying cow! She just didn't want me. Well, I made her want me. I showed her how much she wanted me.

But she hit me ... hurt me ... and now I've got to go and find another love of my life.

I heard the door open. Shit!

"Henry, are you home? Are you okay?"

"Hi Mommy," I reply, sweetness in my voice. "I'm fine How was your day?"

"It was hard," Mommy replied as she walked into the kitchen. I turned and saw her dishevelled waitress uniform. "You know what that place is like."

"I hate you working there," I snarled as I took a step towards her.

Mommy glanced past me at the corpse in the cupboard.

"Oh no, Henry, not again." I could feel the disappointment dripping in her voice. My lip curled and my fists clenched.

"Oh honey, I didn't mean it like that," Mommy said. "Let's get rid of this one, and then we can go and find you a new girlfriend."

I smiled and knew that as long as my Mommy was here, I wouldn't wake up alone on many days. Just the occasional.

Jessica would stop me from waking up alone. At least... for now.

Jilted

By

S.J.Gibbs

Alone in the desert there is no option but to start to walk, but where will my journey end?

I wake and find I am alone in the middle of the desert.

My heart races and my breath comes quickly.

Surprise trickles through me. I should have stayed with the others of course, but I hate being part of a pack. I'd wandered off, the very thing they'd told us not to do.

A dark feeling ushers in. A sad silence surrounds me.

There I s no option but to start to walk.

The thought comes to me with a disconcerting suddenness, as I recall the advice leaflet, which had been handed to me, the first rule being do not wander away from camp, especially at night.

We'd driven to the camp in buggy's, there would be tracks from there if they'd left without me, but firstly I need to figure it out, which way I'd walked from my tent, before I'd laid down to watch the clear sky and the stars, when I must have fallen asleep.

As I stand, my 6ft. 5in frame feels even taller than usual.

How am I going to survive this? The morning heat is already sizzling. I'm already wishing there was water to swim in.

Why hadn't I at least told somebody I was venturing out for a little while?

This was a disaster of epic proportions. I start my journey at a lope, mainly because I have no sense of direction; I have no idea, which way I came. It all looks the same and the night winds have covered my footsteps.

Out here, you could go batty in no time, of that I'm sure. I walk for what feels like a few miles and none of the scenery changes, it's a horrifying prospect.

I'm already hungry enough to eat my own arm. I sip a tiny amount of water from my canteen, at least I'd had the sense to carry one of those full to the brim when I'd left.

Will they even realize I'm missing? Are they looking for me? I've no idea. Although part of the group, I'd barely spoken to anyone, a loner you see. My tent gives me hope, nobody would be there to pack it away, surely they counted the number of guests they brought out here?

I'm walking but my brain isn't responding.

A sand storm is blowing in front of me I change direction.

To avoid it is the only thing that matters at the moment.

My dark eyes sweep over the horizon, lingering, searching.

I take a few more sips of water.

The camp must be not may miles away, surely I hadn't ventured so far?

It must be the case that the news is out, a man is missing.

Travelling into the desert had sounded like a good chance to get away from everything, from the memories and going off on my own in the night, had put those thoughts even further from my mind.

My wedding day should have been filled with hugs, dancing and joy but instead the love of my life had left me standing at the altar, jilted, and heartbroken. I wanted to hate her, but it was difficult when I loved her so much.

Her explanation had been she had nothing to offer, no excuse, she was just sorry. My voice is low and gentle as I begin to talk to myself; "She's left me with so many questions unanswered. Why would she want to do that to me? She'd even smiled at me when she'd said sorry."

I glance at the tattoo on my forearm, her name permanently inked as a reminder, 'Lizzie.'

She's hurt me so badly. I can't fix it. I'm lost and desperate in the desert but I've been this way anyway, in the world I know.

If I'm honest with myself wandering off during the night had been an excellent idea. Not that I want to die but I don't want to live either.

I'd just plunged into it, it wasn't a deliberate choice, but I guess part of me knew what the outcome was likely to be.

People would think that I'm crazy, maybe I am? I move along faster now, my direction no longer matters to me.

I have a quiet regret but I no longer feel uneasy.

Is that apple pie I smell? The hallucinations are starting of that I'm aware. I swig at my canteen, the last of the water.

I'm overwhelmed by loneliness, but it's not a new feeling. I remember a question she'd asked, "Why id you sleep with my best friend?"

I'd paused before my reply, and in Lizzie's eyes that had been enough to prove my guilt. I'd shaken my head sadly, pointing out with an expression that I wasn't to blame, that I hadn't, and stating what a bad state of things it was that she could even believe such a thing.

Although she'd said she believed me and wanted to still go ahead with the wedding, I'd felt like I was gripping the steering wheel of a vehicle as it plunged head first over a cliff.

I've travelled many miles now through the desert, and I'm becoming impatient that Lizzie hasn't joined me for company.

My phone rings although it isn't very loud.

So the vehicle has gone over the edge of the cliff with me in it.

What an awkward position to be left in, standing at an altar with no bride. I don't want this kind of life, but time is running out, I won't survive much longer.

She's with me now she holds my hand. I'm silent, uncertain what to say to her. I stumble and fall into the sand, the spirits are dancing around me now, my parents, my sister, an old friend, all calling me, waiting for me.

Bird's sing, I push forward towards them, I won't pull back, I let go of Lizzie's hand. My ambition now is different; I'm moving into another dimension, I'm leaving this world. I'm gone; I leave behind my human corpse to rot.

A message from the authors

We all hope that you have enjoyed our tales of fiction and our experiments into genres unknown at times. As it was mentioned at the start, we all started these homeworks with a sense of trepidation, but have now incorporated them into our writing experiences, taking on board the learning curves, and even taking some of the pieces and expanding them into longer stories.

We recommend the writing prompt books as useful tools for any budding writer, and hope that by sharing our own experiences, it will help people take the plunge, to open up a blank word document or pick up a pen and paper and take that first step into their own writing careers.

Good luck and best wishes

J.M., Michael and S.J.

Works Published by the Authors

J.M. McKenzie

Wait For Me

Trident Edge

My Rachel (With S.J. Gibbs)

Puschkinia

Each Usiage

Michael Andrews

For The Lost Soul

The Empty Chair

The Alex Hayden Chronicles

Book 1: Under A Blood Moon

Book 2: The Howling Wind

Book 3: The Cauldron of Fire

Book 4: Dragonfire

Book 5: Children of the Sun

Being Alex Hayden

S.J. Gibbs

My Rachel (With J.M. McKenzie)

The Cutting Edge

A Parallel Persona

Fighting A Battle With Himself

The Secrets to Healing with Clear Crystal Quarts (With D.P. Adams)

Printed in Great Britain
by Amazon